"I thought it was GREAT!!!!! What could be better than a book about a VERY VERY VERY daring, brave, adventurous girl and her best friend who does CRAZY FUN STUFF."
Katy, age 8, Beaufort Street Books

"Fans of Pippi Longstocking will love it."
Little Button Diaries

"Makes the world a better place with peals of laughter and inspirational generosity."
We Love This Book

"Parr is sitting right alongside the best…
This book is simply a delight."
Fallen Star Stories

"A wonderful life-affirming book."
Books for Keeps

"Absolutely hilarious, fabulous characters and a few little sad bits make this book one of my favourite reads this year."
Library Mice

"A truly enchanting book that is sure to become a firm favourite with children."
Outside/In World

"A heartbreaking, heartmaking, hilariously funny tale…
This really is a tremendous book."
Playing by the Book

"The kind of book that a child will treasure … a real gem."
The School Librarian

Waffle Hearts

Lena and Me in Mathildewick Cove

MARIA PARR

Translated from Norwegian by Guy Puzey

WALKER
BOOKS

First published in Great Britain 2013 by Walker Books Ltd
87 Vauxhall Walk, London SE11 5HJ

This edition published 2014

10 9 8 7 6 5 4 3 2

This translation has been published with the financial support
of NORLA

This book has been typeset in Berkeley Oldstyle

Printed and bound in Great Britain by Clays Ltd, St Ives plc

British Library Cataloguing in Publication Data:
a catalogue record for this book is available from
the British Library

ISBN 978-1-4063-4790-6

www.walker.co.uk

Contents

Contents

CHAPTER ONE
The hole in the hedge

O n the first afternoon of the summer
holidays, Lena and I made a ropeway
between our houses. Lena, as usual, had to be
the first to try it. She clambered boldly up onto
the window ledge, took hold of the rope with
both hands and swung her two bare feet in a knot
around it. It looked dreadfully dangerous. I held
my breath as she pulled herself across towards her
house, further and further away from the window.
Lena is almost nine years old, and not as strong as

those who are a bit bigger. About halfway, her feet slipped down from the rope with a small "ritsch" sound, and suddenly she was dangling by just her hands between the upstairs floors of the two houses. My heart began to pound really fast.

"Uh-oh," said Lena.

"Keep going!" I yelled.

I was told that it was not as easy to keep going as it might look to someone staring from the window.

"Hang on then! I'll save you!"

My hands started to sweat while I was thinking. I hoped that Lena's hands were dry. What if she lost her grip and fell straight down from a two-storey height? That was when I came up with the idea of the mattress.

So while Lena held on as best as she could, I heaved the mattress off Mum and Dad's bed, shoved it onto the landing, threw it down the stairs, pushed it into the downstairs corridor, opened the front door, kicked it down the doorsteps and dragged it out into the garden. It was a really heavy mattress. On the way I knocked down a picture of my great-great-grandmother, which smashed. Still, it was better that she was broken than Lena.

When I finally came out into the garden, I could see from the grimaces Lena was making that she was close to falling.

"Trille, you slowcoach!" she huffed angrily. Her black pigtails were waving in the wind all the way up there. I acted as if I hadn't heard. She was hanging right over the hedge. I had no choice but to put the mattress there, on top of the hedge.

And then Lena Lid could finally let go, coming tumbling down from the sky like an overripe apple. She landed with a soft crack. Two of the branches in the hedge snapped instantly.

I collapsed on the lawn, relieved, while I watched Lena in the demolished hedge, scrambling furiously between the branches and the fitted sheet.

"That was your fault, Trille, you stupid smoked haddock," she said, getting up uninjured.

It was hardly my fault, I thought, but I didn't say so. I was just glad she was alive. As usual.

CHAPTER TWO
Trille lad and the little lass
from next door

We are in the same class, Lena and I. Lena is the only girl. Luckily it was the summer holidays, otherwise Lena was so fed up with school that she would have fallen into a coma and "popped her clogs", as she puts it.

"Actually, you could've popped your clogs when you fell if there hadn't been a mattress underneath you," I said to her later that evening, when we were back outside looking at the hole in the hedge. Lena

doubted that. She thought she would have got concussion at the most, and she's had that before. Twice.

But I still wonder what would have happened if she had fallen down without a mattress there. It would have been awful if she had kicked the bucket. I wouldn't have Lena any more. She's my best friend, even if she is a girl. I have never told her. I don't dare, as I don't know if I am *her* best friend. Sometimes I think I am, and sometimes I think I'm not. It depends. But I do wonder about it. Especially when things happen like she falls down from ropeways onto mattresses that I have put there; then I think I would like her to tell me that I am her best friend. She doesn't need to say it loudly or anything. She could just say it hidden behind a cough. But she never does. Sometimes it seems that Lena has a heart of stone.

As well as her heart of stone, Lena has green eyes and seven freckles on her nose. She is thin.

Grandpa sometimes says that she eats like a horse and looks like a bicycle. Everyone beats her at arm-wrestling. But Lena says that's because everyone cheats. As for me, I look normal, I think, with light hair and a dimple on one side. It's my name that isn't normal, but that can't be seen on the outside. Mum and Dad named me Theobald Rodrik. They regretted it afterwards. It's not a good idea to give a small baby such a big name. But what's done is done. I've now been called Theobald Rodrik Danielsen Yttergård for nine years. That's quite a while. It's my whole life. Luckily everyone calls me Trille, so I don't really bother about it, apart from when Lena sometimes asks:

"What is it you're called again, Trille?"

Then I answer, "Theobald Rodrik."

And then Lena laughs long and hard. Sometimes she slaps her thigh too.

* * *

The hedge that Lena and I made a hole in marks the boundary between our gardens. The small, white house on one side is where Lena lives with her mother. They don't have a dad in their home, though Lena thinks there would be plenty of space for one if they tidied up the cellar a bit. The big, orange house on the other side is where I live. We have three floors plus an attic, because there are so many people in my family: Mum, Dad, Minda, who's 14, Magnus, who's 13, me, 9, and Krølla, 3. Plus Grandpa, Dad's dad, who has a flat in the basement. That's just enough people to keep under control, says Mum. When Lena comes over it's a little too many, and then things get chaotic.

Today Lena thought it would be a good idea to go into my kitchen to see if anyone had decided to have some coffee and biscuits.

Grandpa had. Every now and then he comes up the stairs from the basement to have a cup of coffee. Grandpa is thin and wrinkly, and has wispy hair. He is the best grown-up I know.

Grandpa kicked off his wooden shoes and stuck his hands in his boiler-suit pockets. He always wears a boiler suit, my grandpa.

"Well, if it isn't Trille lad, and the little lass from next door," he said, bowing. "It looks like we've come on the same mission."

Mum was in the living room reading the newspaper. She hadn't noticed that we'd come in. That's because it's entirely normal for Lena and Grandpa to be in our kitchen, even though neither of them lives here. They just pop in. Lena visits so often that she's almost her own neighbour.

Grandpa picked up a torch that was lying on the kitchen worktop and crept up on Mum.

"Hands up!" he shouted, pretending that the torch was a pistol. "Stand and deliver! Your coffee or your life, Lady Kari."

"And biscuits!" Lena added, just to make sure.

Lena, Grandpa and I, we get coffee and biscuits almost whenever we want. Mum isn't capable of saying no. At least not when we ask for it nicely. And certainly not when her life is threatened with a torch.

We're a nice bunch, I thought, as the four of us sat around the kitchen table eating biscuits and messing around. Mum had been pretty cross about the ropeway, but now she was smiling again, and suddenly she asked if Lena and I were looking forward to being Midsummer bride and groom.

Lena stopped her munching. "This year as well? Are you planning to marry the two of us to death?"

"No," Mum protested, she was not planning to marry us to death, but Lena cut her off, saying that was exactly what she was doing.

"You're trying to finish us off! We refuse to do it," she insisted, without asking me first. But that was OK. I had a good mind to refuse to do it as well. It's always Lena and me who have to dress up as the traditional Midsummer bride and groom.

"It's no good asking us, Mum," I said. "Can't we do something else?"

Mum didn't have a chance to say another word before Lena made a dramatic suggestion: she and I could make the witch to put on the bonfire. I was stunned. But then I felt happy. Minda and Magnus made the Midsummer witch every year. It was only fair to let Lena and me have a try for once. Lena begged and pleaded, and then shook Mum's hand while jumping up and down.

"Let Trille lad and the little lass make the witch. Another bride and groom will turn up," said Grandpa.

And that's how Lena and I got our first witch-making assignment. It will most likely be our last too.

CHAPTER THREE
Dousing a witch

We live in a small bay called
Mathildewick Cove, Lena and I.
Grandpa says Mathildewick Cove is a kingdom.
Grandpa mostly makes things up, but I like to
think that he's right this time: Mathildewick Cove
is our kingdom. Between our houses and the sea
we have some big fields, and there's a small gravel
track that goes above those fields down to the
shore. By the track grow rowan trees, which we
climb in when the wind blows. Every morning

when I get up, I look out of my window at the sea and at the weather. When the wind is really blowing, the waves come crashing over the jetty and the spray goes far up onto the fields. When it's not windy, the sea looks like an enormous puddle. If you look carefully, you notice that the sea is a different shade of blue each day. I always look for Grandpa's boat too. He gets up at five o'clock every morning to go fishing.

Above our houses there's the main road, and above the main road there are slopes to go tobogganing or skiing on in winter. Once, Lena and I made a ramp so that Lena could try jumping over the main road on her toboggan. She landed right in the middle of the road and hurt her backside so badly that she had to lie on her stomach for two days. There was a car coming too. It had to jam on its brakes before we could roll her onto the verge.

At the top of the slopes, far, far up, is Hillside

Jon's farm. He's Grandpa's best friend. Further up from there are the mountains and, when you get to the top of the mountains, you can see our little cabin. It takes two hours to walk there.

Lena and I know everything that's worth knowing about Mathildewick Cove. And even more. So we knew exactly where we should look to find what we needed for the witch.

Thank goodness Grandpa has taught us how to make proper knots. It comes in handy every so often, even if we have solemnly sworn not to make any more ropeways. Before you could say "smoking haddocks", Lena had tied a clove hitch so that our witch would stay together. Lena is really fast when she gets going. But it still took us a long time to get the hay to stop sticking out of the old rags we put around it. The witch was quite limp: it wasn't easy to straighten her up. She was as big as Lena and me, and looked scary enough.

We took a few steps back and tilted our heads.

"Excellent," said Lena, smiling contentedly.

Just when we were going to put the witch in the old stables, along came Magnus.

"Have you made a scarecrow?" he asked.

"It's a witch," I explained.

Magnus began to laugh. "That thing there? That's the most rubbish witch I've ever seen! Good thing it's going to be burnt!"

I got quite angry. Lena got even angrier.

"Clear off! Just go down to the shore and build the bonfire!" she yelled, so loudly that my jumper quivered.

So Magnus left, but we could hear him laughing for a long time. I told Lena that Magnus was just jealous because it's usually he and Minda who make the witch. But that didn't help much. Lena snarled and kicked the witch, making her fall over. A bit of hay came out through her stomach.

We went to Lena's and made some squash. Lena's mother paints and makes art out of strange things, so their whole house is filled with all kinds of odd objects. They even have half a motorbike in their utility room. It'll be a whole bike when they finish screwing it all together. Lena blew big, angry bubbles in her glass as her eyes darted around the living room. All of a sudden she stopped blowing and her face took on a thoughtful look.

Up on top of a red corner cupboard was the biggest doll I'd ever seen. I'd often looked at it. Her hands were loose and a bit of the paint on her face had peeled off, but Lena's mum had decorated her with dried flowers. It was the doll that Lena was looking at.

I was terrified when I realized what she was thinking.

"But surely we can't...?"

"Witches are supposed to be made of old junk, Trille. Smoking haddocks, that doll is over seventy years old; Mum has said so many times."

"Isn't it *too* old?" I asked.

Lena thought that was a good question, even if she did say so herself. The older, the better. She pushed the yellow rocking chair over to the cupboard and ordered me up to get the doll down.

"My knees are shaking," I mumbled.

Lena grabbed hold of them with her lean fingers. "They're not now."

It was easier to make a witch when we had a doll inside instead of hay. With a nose made from a Yule goat decoration, as well as sunglasses and a headscarf, she almost looked alive. Nobody would have guessed it was a doll. We hid her under Lena's bed.

* * *

It took me a while to get to sleep that night. In the end I included the witch in my evening prayers.

"Dear God, please don't let her get really burnt up."

When I came down to the kitchen on the morning of the Midsummer festival, Auntie Granny was there.

"Well, if it isn't my young laddie Trille," she said with a wink.

Auntie Granny is fat and old, and is Grandpa's big sister. She lives about twelve miles away and comes to visit us every time it's not an ordinary day – at Christmas and Easter and on birthdays, and on 17 May, the national day, and so on. And at Midsummer. Our real grandmother, who was married to Grandpa, died when she was only thirty-five. Auntie Granny is our substitute grandmother.

I felt all warm inside when I saw her. Auntie Granny's face is such a nice shape because she smiles the whole time. Everyone in my family is cheerful and makes jokes when she comes to visit, and we play ludo and eat boiled sweets and listen to stories told by Auntie Granny and Grandpa. And Auntie Granny makes waffles. People say that lots of things are the best in the world, but Auntie Granny's waffles really *are* the best in the world, seriously.

It was a beautiful day. Even Dad joined in with the games and waffle-eating. He was supposed to be muck-spreading, but Mum thought that he should wait for another day so that we wouldn't have to celebrate Midsummer surrounded by the smell of manure. And Dad thought that was absolutely fine.

At six o'clock, Mum clapped her hands and said it was time for the bonfire. I wished I had a button on my forehead that I could press to make me disappear. Why didn't God make buttons like that for us? I'd much rather have that than those toes in the middle that don't do anything.

We were just about to go, when Auntie Granny put her hand on her back and said that she had to have a little rest. Grandpa stayed to keep her company – and to eat even more boiled sweets and waffles.

"I want to stay here too!" I said.

I wasn't allowed.

I hadn't seen Lena all day, but here she came with our magnificent witch wrapped up in a sheet, and with a deep worry line on her forehead.

"Shall we just forget about it?" I said.

Lena glanced quickly at Magnus and shook her head.

Everyone who lives in Mathildewick Cove was gathered down on the shore. There was my family, Lena's mother, Uncle Tor, who is Dad's little brother, and Uncle Tor's girlfriend. On the pebbles was the tallest and best bonfire I'd ever seen. Minda, Magnus and Dad had built it. My older sister and brother were happy and proud.

"Well, now all that's missing is the witch," smiled Dad, twirling his moustache.

Lena cleared her throat and rolled the witch out of the sheet. Everyone stared in amazement at what we'd made.

"That's brilliant," said Minda, impressed, and the grown-ups nodded. Out of the corner of my eye, I saw that Lena's worry line had turned into a small crater. I checked my own forehead. There was no button yet.

Minda took the witch under her arm and clambered up to the top of the bonfire. Her knees didn't shake in the slightest while she was up there – several metres above ground level. Minda was adopted from Colombia. Mum and Dad adopted her when she was a little orphaned baby.

I sometimes wonder if she isn't really an Inca princess. She looks a bit like one. And on this Midsummer's Eve, when she was standing on top of the bonfire with her hair fluttering in the wind, I thought she looked more like an Inca princess than ever. I almost felt happy for a moment, until Uncle Tor pulled out his lighter. He was just about to light the fire when Krølla shouted:

"Bwide and gwoom!"

Everyone turned round. There was a couple dressed as bride and groom coming across our freshly cut field. Grandpa and Auntie Granny! I think I went into a mild state of shock. It was the kind of thing you only see in films. Auntie Granny had borrowed Dad's suit and was dressed as the bridegroom. She looked like a fat penguin. And Grandpa was wearing a long, white dress, a veil and high-heeled shoes. He was using his cactus as the wedding bouquet.

I didn't know it was possible to laugh like we did then. Mum's fizzy pear juice went down the wrong way so much that she coughed until the next day. Uncle Tor had to kneel down, he was laughing so much. And the best thing of all was that nobody was thinking about the bonfire.

But when Grandpa and Auntie Granny finally sat down, Uncle Tor took out his lighter again.

"Don't light it," Lena said quickly.

Everyone looked at her in surprise, but before we could protest any more, Uncle Tor had set it alight. I saw Lena stop breathing for a moment. She was gathering strength for a gigantic scream: the sort of scream that only Lena can produce. I just managed to put my hands over my ears before it came.

"PUT IT OUT!" she howled.

The flames were dancing up the side of the bonfire towards the witch.

"Mum, it's your doll! It's your doll that's inside the witch. Put it out!"

Minda was the first to react. As fast as lightning, she emptied a tin of sausages and filled it with sea water. Then it was as if everyone woke up. We emptied all the tins and boxes we could find and tripped over each other on our way to and from the water's edge. Dad pointed and gave orders and tried to get us to form a line. He's a member of the volunteer fire brigade in our area. But it wasn't much use. The flames were eating their way up.

"Oh no, oh no," I groaned quietly, no longer daring to look at the bonfire.

We eventually realized that we couldn't douse it. The bonfire was raging.

"It's no use," shouted Uncle Tor, throwing his arms out.

Just as he said that and all hope was lost, we heard someone starting the tractor. It was still up in the field with a spreader full of manure. Grandpa had got in and was reversing towards us at a furious speed.

"Out of the way!" he yelled from the window, trying to keep the veil out of his eyes.

Mum gave a shriek. That was all she could do before the bride turned the muck-spreader on full-pelt, at just the right distance from the bonfire.

For a short, bizarre moment the sky turned brown. I remember thinking, There's no way this can be happening! Everyone bent over with their hands above their heads. Then the cowpats came raining down. Every single one of us was sprayed with muck from head to toe. It was no use running. We couldn't see or hear anything other than flying muck.

When it finally stopped, it was as if all the sounds in the world had gone. Everyone, all the people from Mathildewick Cove, just stood there.

Not an inch of our bodies was free of cow muck. In my whole life I will never, ever forget it.

The tractor door opened slowly. Grandpa carefully lifted his dazzling white dress up a little and tiptoed neatly through the muck towards us.

"Oh well," he said, and nodded at the bonfire.

There was not a flame to be seen. The bonfire and the witch were just as covered in manure as we were.

"Thank you, Grandpa," I said quietly.

CHAPTER FOUR
Noah's Shark

The day afterwards, we went to Sunday school, Lena and I. We took Krølla with us too.

It had rained that night, so there were lots of puddles on the road. Krølla had her wellies on the wrong feet and had to be dragged along the uphill stretches.

"Thank goodness she's not my sister," said Lena every time she had to wait for us, but I knew that she didn't mean it deep inside. Krølla is as good as gold. Actually, she's called something as strange as I am. Konstanse Lillefine or something. I can't really remember.

At Sunday school we learnt about Noah's Ark. Noah was a man who lived several thousand years ago in another country. He built a big boat called the Ark on top of a mountain. It was God who had said that Noah should build his boat on top of the mountain. It was going to start to rain in a major way, God said. The whole Earth would become an ocean. Noah had to gather together a male and a female of all the animals that existed and take them aboard the Ark before the rain started, otherwise they would drown. People thought that it was very strange of Noah to put those animals in a boat on top of a mountain, but Noah didn't care. When he'd finished, it began to rain. First the water covered the fields and the roads, then it flooded over the treetops and houses, and eventually it rose all the way up to the mountain where Noah and the Ark were.

The water lifted the big boat up from the mountain top. Noah sailed around in the Ark together with his family and the animals for several weeks. The terrible thing was that anyone who wasn't aboard the Ark drowned. God also thought that was sad, so afterwards he made a rainbow and promised that he would never again pour so much rain down at once.

When we were walking home in the sunshine, Lena said, "Ark is a pretty stupid name for a boat. That Noah could've thought up a better one."

"Who says it was Noah who thought up the name?" I said, jumping over a large puddle.

"Who was it, then?" asked Lena, jumping over an even larger puddle. "Did they make a mistake in the Bible?"

"They didn't make mistakes in the Bible, did they?" I said, getting ready to jump over the largest puddle of all. I landed in the middle of it.

"Maybe they hadn't invented all the letters of the alphabet yet," said Lena after the splash. "Since it was donkey's years ago."

While I was emptying the water out of mine and Krølla's wellies, I asked Lena if she had a better name for the boat. Lena didn't answer straight away. I thought she wasn't going to come up with anything, but then:

"Shark."

Noah's Shark.

Everyone here in Norway knows that a shark (or *sjark*, as we spell it) is a kind of fishing boat. An ark is something else, like that big chest in Indiana Jones. Lena gave a resigned sigh, thinking of the people who had written the Bible so carelessly.

"Shark boats aren't exactly very big," I said.

Lena shook her head. "Well, that's why the dinosaurs died out, Trille. They drowned. Noah didn't have space for them."

It was at that very moment, while I was imagining how Noah would have pushed and struggled trying to get a Tyrannosaurus Rex aboard, that I had my brilliant idea:

"Lena, why don't we try it with a shark? Let's see how many animals we have space for!"

There was nothing Lena would rather spend her Sunday doing than precisely that.

Uncle Tor has a beautiful big shark boat that he uses every day except Sunday. He is easily angered, Uncle Tor, especially by Lena and me. But shark boats aren't just scattered around everywhere. You have to be content with whichever shark you can find, even if it's Tor's, said Lena. Would Noah have worried about a slightly difficult uncle when the whole world was at stake? We dropped off Krølla with Dad and ran on.

*   *   *

Uncle Tor lives in the third, and last, house in Mathildewick Cove, right down by the sea. That Sunday he had gone to the cinema in town. The shark was there, bobbing by the jetty. All we had to do was climb aboard and put down the gangplank. I'd done it before because I'd been out fishing on it once. We put on lifejackets, and suddenly that made us feel better about taking a shark without asking. For a moment we also discussed taking our cycling helmets, but we decided not to.

There are quite a lot of different animals in Mathildewick Cove. Some small ones and some big ones. First we carried down the two rabbits that live outside Grandpa's kitchen window. They're called February and March. It was impossible to get them to stay still on deck, but when we gave them an armful of dandelion leaves, they calmed down. Afterwards, we went into the chicken run behind our hay barn and took one of the hens, Number

Four to be precise, and our cockerel. The cockerel made a terrible racket. For a moment we were sure that Mum would hear us, but I think the radio must have been on inside. The sheep are up the mountain in the summer, so we had to make do with our only goat. She's the same age as Magnus and has a difficult temperament, as Auntie Granny says. When the stupid goat came aboard the boat, she ate all the rabbits' dandelions, so we had to pick some more. After that, we searched all over Mathildewick Cove for our two cats, but could only find Festus.

"He's so fat he can count as two," said Lena, putting him down in the sun by the boat's cabin.

Our lifejackets had become loose from all that carrying. We tightened them up properly, fetched as many jam jars as we could carry from the larder, then started on the insects. We managed to catch two bumble-bees, two worms, two snails, two greenflies, two spiders and two beetles. Six jars altogether. Hours had passed by the time we'd finished. We were hungry and our backs ached. One of the bumble-bees had even stung Lena when she tried to find out if it was a boy bee or a girl bee.

"We're never going to finish," she said, rubbing furiously at the sting.

I looked at all the animals lying nicely in the sun on the deck. I had never seen animals on a boat before. Maybe they'd spent their whole lives wishing that they could have a boat ride. That was a beautiful thought.

But there was still space for more.

Lena looked at me earnestly.

"Trille, it's time we got a cow."

Uncle Tor has heifers. Heifers are adolescent cattle that are a little more restless than ordinary cattle and have slightly smaller udders. They were put out to graze above my uncle's house. Everything we need belongs to Uncle Tor, I thought, wishing that we had our own cattle. He was going to go mad. My knees were shaking, and I showed Lena.

"You've got to do something about those knees of yours, Trille!" she said.

Lena thought that Tor would understand. After all, we couldn't keep on wearing ourselves out with insects all day. We had to have an animal that took up some space. I wasn't so sure Uncle Tor would understand, but I didn't say anything.

We stood for a while looking at the grazing heifers, then chose the one that looked biggest and best behaved.

"Come on, Miss Moo," said Lena, carefully taking hold of the collar round the heifer's neck.

And she did. She followed us down to the jetty without the slightest commotion. It was like leading a very big and well-behaved dog.

"Now it's going to be full!" said Lena, satisfied.

My knees calmed down. Lena and I had done the same as Noah. We had filled a shark with animals. All we had left to do was get this heifer on board.

But in the middle of the gangplank, with the heifer in front of us, we suddenly discovered that the goat was eating the curtains in the cabin. Lena let out a furious scream, and from that moment everything went wrong...

The heifer was so scared by Lena's scream that she jumped almost half a metre up in the air and leapt onto the shark with a crash. She mooed madly into the sky and kicked out in all directions. The cat and the rabbits began to scurry everywhere. Number Four and the cockerel flew up and down, clucking and crowing. The goat looked around in surprise and pooped on the deck. And as if that wasn't enough, the heifer slipped on the goat's droppings and kicked the window with the half-eaten curtain, smashing it. Everything was a complete mess of feathers and dung and dandelions and rabbits.

Lena and I stood there, our arms hanging by our sides, just staring. In the end, the heifer jumped into the sea with a majestic splash.

Then along came Uncle Tor. Lucky for the heifer. Unlucky for us.

"What the heck is all this mayhem?" he shouted, so loudly that I'm sure they heard him in Colombia.

"We learnt it at Sunday school," shrieked Lena.

The heifer was thrashing around in the sea like a little brown motor boat. She must have been afraid of water. Uncle Tor said nothing. He jumped up into the boat and made a lasso out of a rope that was lying there.

He's no cowboy, my uncle, and he had to throw the lasso many times before he got the loop round the heifer's head. When he finally pulled her ashore, he was wet and angry and he was foaming with rage.

"You hooligans!" he roared.

I was relieved he had to stay exactly where he was, holding the heifer.

"Trille Danielsen Yttergård! Lena Lid! If either of you so much as sets foot on my property in the next six months, I will bash your heads right down into your stomachs!" he snarled, waving us away so forcefully that his arm almost fell off his shoulder.

We ran for all we were worth, flinging ourselves down behind Krølla's Wendy house. For a while I lay on my back in despair. Eventually Lena said, "If you had your head in your stomach, then you could still see through your belly button."

Parents always spot when you've done something wrong. It was the same this time. It's like they've got a built-in radar. Mum and Dad and Lena's mum dragged us straight into our kitchen and demanded to be told what we had been up to. We didn't even have a chance to take off our lifejackets.

There was nothing to do but spill the beans and explain everything. When we had finished, the three parents sat there wide-eyed, just looking at us. There was a deathly hush. Lena sighed like she does when we have Maths lessons, a weak, faltering sigh. I drummed my fingers on my lifejacket, so at least they would notice that we had remembered to wear them.

"Now I've *herd* everything," said Dad at last, trying to hide a smile under his moustache.

Mum looked at him sternly. It was no time for jokes in her view.

"Are you two completely out of your minds?" she asked.

I didn't know what to answer, so I just nodded.

Even I could see things had gone a little too far this weekend.

"You'll have to go down there, say sorry and bring the animals back up," Lena's mum said firmly.

"I think Tor would prefer not to see us," mumbled Lena.

But it was no use. Dad strode down in his wooden shoes, dragging us with him. In spite of everything, I was glad that he was going with us. Uncle Tor is his little brother. It helps to remember that on days like this.

"You are totally nuts, Trille!" shouted Magnus from the attic as we went outside. I acted as if I hadn't heard him.

"Now might have been a good time to wear our cycling helmets," I muttered to Lena.

There was no rainbow in the sky that day, even though Lena and I had filled an entire shark with animals. But it didn't rain either. It was OK in the end. Uncle Tor's girlfriend was visiting, and she's fond of children, even ones like Lena and me. Uncle Tor couldn't stay really angry as long as she was there.

"We will never borrow your boat or your heifer again without asking," said Lena.

"And we'll pay for the broken window,"
I promised.

Lena looked at me and coughed.

"When we can afford it," I added.

Afterwards, Uncle Tor's girlfriend gave us apple pie and custard.

By the time we had put the animals back where they belonged, the grass was covered with dew. Lena whistled quietly.

"You know which things rhyme, Trille?"

I shook my head.

"Miss Moo and poo!" She grinned.

Then she ran laughing through the hole in the hedge. I heard her slam her front door shut. She always does that. She slams it so hard it can be heard all over Mathildewick Cove.

That's just what she's like, Lena Lid.

CHAPTER FIVE
Wanted: a dad

The next day, Dad began his summer project. He has one every year. The project is generally something large and difficult to build, and it's always Mum who decides what that is. This year, Mum had decided that we should have a stone wall above the paved part of our garden. Lena was delighted. She loves balancing on walls.

"Please make it high and narrow," she ordered.

Dad grunted from between the stones. He doesn't like his summer projects. He would rather sit on the balcony drinking coffee. We hadn't been standing there watching him laying stones for long before he asked us to run far, far away and play.

When we had run through the hedge into Lena's garden and gone up to her wall, I asked, "Hey, Lena, why don't you have a dad?" and then quickly tried to cover up the question with a nervous cough.

"I do have a dad," Lena answered.

She held her arms straight out as she walked backwards, balancing on the wall. I watched her worn-out tennis shoes move further and further away.

"Where is he, then?"

Lena didn't know. He'd done a runner before she was born.

"He did a runner?" I asked in dismay.

"Can't you hear?" Lena looked at me, irritated. Then she burst out, "What use are they, anyway?"

I didn't really know what to answer. Do they need a use?

"They build things," I suggested. "Walls and so on."

Lena had a wall.

"And then they can … um…"

I'd never thought properly about what use my dad was. To get ideas, I stretched up onto my toes and peeped over the hedge. Dad was standing there muttering about his summer project, red in the face. It wasn't too easy to come up with exactly what use he was.

"They eat boiled cabbage," I said in the end.

Neither Lena nor I like boiled cabbage. It tastes like slime. Unfortunately we have a whole field of cabbages in Mathildewick Cove. Both my mum and Lena's mum say that cabbage is something we should eat, for our own good. But Dad doesn't say so. He eats my cabbage. I just heave the green glob over onto his plate when Mum's looking the other way.

I could see that Lena didn't think that was such a silly suggestion. She had a good view of Dad and his summer project from up there on the wall. She stood on one foot for a long while, studying him thoroughly.

"Hm," she said eventually, jumping down.

Later in the day we went to the General Store to buy the things that Magnus had forgotten. Lena's mum works there. She was in the middle of counting tins of sweetcorn when we arrived.

"Hi!" she called out.

"Hi," I said.

Lena just lifted her hand and waved.

When we came back out, we stopped to read the adverts on the door, like we always do. Today there was an extra big one. We leant down closer.

> WANTED: A PUPPY.
>
> MIXED-BREEDS WELCOME.
>
> MUST BE HOUSE-TRAINED.

Lena read the card over and over.

"Do you want a dog?" I asked.

"No, but surely it must be possible to do something similar for dads too?"

Magnus had once told Lena and me about personal ads. They're the kind of adverts you put in the newspapers when you want to find a boyfriend or girlfriend. Lena had thought a bit about it, she told me. When it came to this dad thing, would it be possible to write an advert like that for a dad? There was just one disadvantage: you never knew who might be reading the paper. It could be gangsters or headmasters or whoever. So it was better to put up her advert at

the General Store, where she knew who would
be shopping.

"You write it, Trille. You're so good at joined-up
writing," she said when she'd been into the shop
to fetch a pen and paper. One of her pigtails was
hanging off to the side at a funny angle, but she
looked very determined. I felt very sceptical.

"What should we write, then?"

Lena lay down on the wooden table outside
the shop and started thinking so hard that I could
almost hear it.

"Write 'Wanted: a dad'," she began.

I sighed. "Lena, don't you think...?"

"Write it!"

I shrugged and did as she said. After that,
Lena went quiet for a long time, by her standards.
At last, she cleared her throat and spoke loudly
and slowly:

"Must be nice and like boiled cabbage, but

anyone welcome as long as he is nice and likes boiled cabbage."

I frowned. It sounded strange.

"Are you sure we should write about cabbage, Lena?"

No, Lena wasn't sure. But he *would* have to be nice.

In the end, the advert looked like this:

Wanted: a dad.
Must be very nise.
And must like childrin.

Right at the top we wrote Lena's phone number, and then she stuck it up, just below the dog advert.

"You're nuts!" I said.

"I am not nuts. I just like to speed things along," answered Lena.

* * *

Lena really had sped things along. Just half an hour after we got back to her house, the phone rang. Actually, I don't think Lena had thought very carefully about what we had done until that moment.

The phone kept on ringing.

"Aren't you going to get it?" I whispered eventually.

She stood reluctantly and picked up the receiver.

"H–hello…?"

Lena's voice was as thin as a piece of thread. I put my ear up to the phone too.

"Hi there. It's Vera Johansen here. Was it you who put up an advert at the General Store?"

Lena looked at me wide-eyed and then coughed: "Yes…"

"Great! Then I've got something that will interest you. He's still a bit nervous, but, you know, he hasn't peed inside once in the past two weeks!"

Lena's chin almost fell down to her stomach. I could see her tonsils.

"Does he pee outside?" asked Lena in alarm.

"Yes, isn't he clever!"

Vera Johansen sounded very proud. She had to be crazy, I thought. A dad who didn't pee inside! Lena's face took on a strange look, but she probably thought she had to pull herself together a bit, so she cleared her throat and asked a little sternly if he liked boiled cabbage. There was silence for a moment at the other end.

"No, actually, I've never fed him that. Is your mum home perhaps? Surely she'd like to have a say in the matter too?"

Lena sank to her knees. Vera Johansen said she would bring him over at five-ish, so we could have a look at him. It would be easier to decide then.

After she had hung up, Lena stayed there, seated, staring into space.

"Does your dad pee outside, Trille?" she asked after a bit.

"Very rarely."

Lena lay down on her stomach and banged her head on the floor.

"Oh, fishcakes! What's Mum going to say?"

We soon found out. The door slammed wide open like a thunderclap, and in came Lena's mother with the advert in her hand and flushed red cheeks. She looked like Lena.

"Lena Lid! What is this?"

Down on the floor, Lena didn't move.

"Answer me! Are you completely mad?"

I noticed Lena didn't have much to say.

"She's trying to speed things along," I explained.

Luckily, Lena's mum is used to being Lena's mum, so she isn't shocked by things like this. I looked at her and thought that there must be a lot of people who would like to marry her. She has a silver nose stud.

"I'll never do it again," Lena promised from down below.

Her mum sat down on the floor too. They tend to do that in their house.

"Oh well. I managed to tear away the card before anyone saw it," she laughed.

I saw that I would have to help out again:

"Vera Johansen is bringing him at five o'clock."

That afternoon, Lena's mum rang Vera Johansen seventeen times. Nobody picked up. The clock was ticking. From quarter to five, all three of us sat around the kitchen table, waiting. The minute hand crept towards the twelve, notch by notch.

"You're making this up," Lena's mum said.

Then the doorbell rang.

A smiling Vera Johansen stood on the doorstep

wearing a red blouse, her head tilted at a friendly angle. We tried to see past her. None of us could spot any dads, but you never can tell. Maybe he was having a pee round the corner.

"Good afternoon," said Lena's mum.

"Good afternoon, good afternoon! Well, now, you must be excited to see what I've brought with me!" said Vera, almost shouting.

Lena's mum tried to smile. Unsuccessfully.

"Actually, we've changed our minds," Lena stammered, but Vera Johansen was already on the way to her car. It's impossible to stop ladies like her.

Lena isn't so easy to stop either, as it happens. She jumped out onto the doorstep and sprinted past Vera.

"Listen, we don't want him! They're supposed to pee indoors!"

Just then, we heard a tiny, delicate bark from the car. A puppy's head appeared in the window.

"A dog?" whispered Lena.

"Yes." Vera Johansen frowned. "Wasn't it a dog you wanted?"

Lena opened and closed her mouth several times.

"No, I wanted…"

"A chinchilla!" her mother shouted from the door.

The puppy that Vera Johansen had brought was sweeter than a chinchilla. Lena wanted to keep him, but, as her mum said, you have to draw the line somewhere. Afterwards, Lena's mum spent a long time fixing the motorbike in order to calm down. Lena and I sat on the washing machine and watched. Now and then she asked us to pass her tools. Otherwise we stayed silent.

"You can't just randomly put up adverts, Lena," her mum said eventually. "Didn't you think about who we might have ended up with?"

I thought about all the bachelors who do their shopping at the General Store.

"Besides, we haven't got space for a dad here," continued her mum, from under the motorbike.

Lena disagreed. They could tidy up the cellar.

"There are enough men in this house already. We've got Trille," her mum insisted.

Lena thought that was the stupidest thing she had heard in a long time.

"Trille's not a man!"

"What am I then?" I asked.

"You're a neighbour."

Uh-huh, I thought, wishing she'd said I was a best friend instead.

CHAPTER SIX

The Battle of Mathildewick Cove

Almost all the grown-ups in our area sing in
the mixed choir. A mixed choir, according
to Dad, is a choir in which everyone is mixed
together, both those who can sing and those who
can't. Dad is the conductor and tries to get them to
sing as nicely as possible. In summer, our mixed
choir goes off and meets other mixed choirs at a
choral festival. Then they all mix together in chorus
and sing for a whole weekend. The choral festival
is so much fun that everyone in our mixed choir

looks forward to it for weeks in advance.

As for the children, we also look forward to it, because all the grown-ups except for Grandpa are away for a whole weekend, and Mum declares a state of emergency in Mathildewick Cove. This summer it would be extra crazy, as Minda and Magnus were going to be away at camp at the same time as the festival. There would be only the little ones and Grandpa left in the whole cove.

"It's going to be a sight to behold," chortled Grandpa when he found out.

"Lars, my dear, that's what worries me," grumbled Mum, who was wondering whether to drop the whole choral festival, out of sheer anxiety at what we might get up to while they were away. Lena, on the other hand, thought it was brilliant. Grandpa was going to babysit her too.

"Thank goodness you sing like a crow that's crashed!" she told him when she and her mother came over to our house the evening before the festival in order to lay down some rules.

It was a long evening. When the grown-ups had finished lecturing Lena, Krølla and me thoroughly and at length about being good and not making ropeways while they were away, it was Grandpa's turn.

"The children must wear lifejackets if they're in a boat and helmets on their bikes. There's bread in the freezer. Our mobile number's above the phone…"

Mum kept on talking. Grandpa kept on nodding.

"… and, Lars, my dear, none of your grandchildren or young neighbours are to ride in your moped box," she said finally. Grandpa didn't nod at that, and I swear I saw his fingers crossed behind his back.

At five past eight the next morning, the sun came in through my window and tickled my nose.

A smell of boiled fish and coffee was coming all the way into my room. Grandpa's smell! I looked out at the sea, which was bright blue with small waves, then I ran downstairs. Krølla and Lena were already sitting at the kitchen counter eating bread with fish and mayonnaise. He only eats fish, my grandpa. That's why the cats are happiest downstairs with him. They share the same favourite dish.

Grandpa spread so much butter on my bread that it looked like cheese.

"Get that grub down you, Trille, my lad. We're going for a ride. You can't see the world from the kitchen table!"

Grandpa's moped looks more or less like a back-to-front tricycle with a big box at the front. Grandpa usually carries things in the box, but when it's the choral festival, grandchildren and neighbours get to have a ride in it.

The first job that day was to pick up two tins of paint that Grandpa had ordered from town. They would be coming across the fjord on the ferry.

We decided we would pretend that the paint tins were full of gold coins. The Royal Mathildan Agents had to hide the tins in Mathildewick Cove, because the deadly Balthazar Gang was after them.

"The pirate king Balthazar will do anything to get his hands on those coins," I said, narrowing my eyes.

"He eats live rabbits whole!" Lena whispered slyly.

"And fish," added Krølla, with eyes as round as saucers.

Not even Mum would have spotted that there were three children, all with their own water pistols, in Grandpa's moped box when we started our journey to the ferry landing. We were huddled at the bottom with a woollen blanket over our heads.

Grandpa's moped rattles almost endlessly. It's like your tongue vibrates inside your mouth when you get on. I was so thrilled with all the excitement that my legs hurt. Finally the moped stopped, and Agent Lena threw off the woollen blanket, which fluttered towards the ferry slip.

"Freeze!" she shouted, pointing her pistol dramatically at the ferry.

There aren't usually all that many people on the ferry. I know that because Dad works there and we go with him for a couple of trips now and then. We expected to see four or five cars and Able Seaman Birger. But not today. Today there was a family reunion at one of the farms, and over twenty old ladies were staring terror-stricken at Lena and me.

"Uh-oh," murmured Grandpa. "Hurry, quick as a flash, and let's get that paint!"

In a panic, I slalomed between all the flowery

skirts, finally reaching Able Seaman Birger and
the paint.

"Th–thanks," I stuttered in a very unconvincing
agent's voice, and snatched the tins from him.
I could hear Mini-Agent Krølla a short distance
away, shouting "bam bam bam" at the poor ferry
passengers.

"It's the whole Balthazar Gang," whispered
Lena excitedly when I had finally completed my
assignment.

"It's Hillside Marie and Ola's wife, Lovise.
I went to confirmation class with them," Grandpa
muttered, lifting his hand to his helmet in a cheerful
salute. Our mini-agent kept on shouting "bam" until
Lena pulled her clattering back down into the box.
Grandpa started the moped with a lurch, and its
rattling was worse than ever as we began our escape
to our fortress back in Mathildewick Cove. It was
like being in an electric mixer.

After a while Lena thought it was safe to remove the woollen blanket. I squinted against the sun. Grandpa was leaning flat over the handlebars, giving the moped full throttle. Occasionally he turned to look behind. I peered past him and saw that we were taking part in a car chase. The roads where we live are narrow, and Grandpa was driving down the middle. It was impossible for cars to overtake. And, even though he was driving as fast as the moped would go, that's not especially fast. Behind us was a whole queue of traffic from the ferry, all going to the family reunion. They hooted and honked. It was like a long parade, with us at the front. I could see Grandpa grinning inside his helmet. He was showing off for his old classmates.

"Hold on tight!" he shouted suddenly. "We're taking a short cut!"

Grandpa made a sharp left turn onto the

old tractor track that cuts across the fields to our house. It was so bumpy I thought I might dislocate something.

"Yee-ha!" shouted Lena as we roared into the farmyard, skidding to a halt and spraying gravel everywhere.

Safely back home, we turned the house into a fortress. Grandpa was our commander-in-chief and went round with a rolling pin under his belt. We put the tins of paint in the middle of the living-room floor, then built defences in front of all the doors to the house, so the Balthazar thieves would never get in. We used almost every single piece of furniture we have. Krølla, who was standing guard, kept shouting that the thieves were coming. Then she would almost scream with laughter when we pretended to shoot out the window, especially when Grandpa used the rolling pin as a bazooka.

"Choral festival is the best," I said to Lena, but Lena thought it would be even more fun if someone really did try to break in.

Then Grandpa suggested inviting Auntie Granny round for a cup of coffee.

"She's here! The old pirate queen," whispered Lena.

We lay as still as statues on a table in Minda's room and peered out the window. Auntie Granny's head was right below us. She rang the doorbell. Lena and I carefully inched our pistols out of the window.

"You're never getting in!"

Lena sounded very fierce, and Auntie Granny looked up in surprise.

"Oh my, Trille darling. Aren't you going to open the door?"

I explained to her briefly that she was a powerful pirate queen. Auntie Granny put her bag down in bewilderment. In a secret compartment inside it there were boiled sweets.

"What about Grandpa, then?" she asked after a moment.

The tip of a rolling pin came into sight through the small bathroom window next to the front door.

"Get lost, Lady Balthazarina!" Grandpa shouted, so loudly that the shower cabinet shook.

Auntie Granny stood in shock for a moment. Then she said something about smoking us out, and vanished.

A long time passed. We couldn't see Auntie Granny anywhere. Lena thought she had gone home, but Grandpa was sure she was up to something and we should keep our guard up. Besides, there were no more buses to Auntie Granny's house.

Then suddenly I smelt something that sent a chill down my spine. I leapt upstairs to the ropeway window with Lena in hot pursuit.

"Smoking haddocks! She's only gone and made waffles!" Lena blurted out.

So she had. Down in Lena's garden, Auntie Granny had equipped herself with a camping table and an electric waffle iron. A long cable trailed away through Lena's kitchen window.

"She's flipping broken into my house!"

Lena was absolutely astonished. There was already a stack of waffles on the table. Now and then, Auntie Granny flapped a tea towel, wafting the smell towards us in great clouds. It gave me goose bumps all over. We stayed as quiet as church mice as we watched the pile of waffles get bigger and bigger. Even Grandpa sat down, disheartened, and looked out the window. None of us was keeping an eye on Krølla. All of a sudden we caught sight of her out in the garden! Auntie Granny gave her a hug and sat her on a sun-lounger. Then she spread butter on a freshly cooked, delicately soft waffle and sprinkled loads of sugar on top. I almost started crying.

"We surrender," Lena said determinedly.

"Suffering sticklebacks, no, we don't!" exclaimed Grandpa, even though Auntie Granny has told him that he's not allowed to say "suffering sticklebacks" when we're listening. "Go to the cellar and fetch your fishing rod, Trille."

Then Grandpa phoned Lena's house. Auntie Granny heard the phone ringing and peered up at us.

"Should I get it?" she asked Lena, who nodded vigorously.

Auntie Granny lifted out the next waffle and disappeared inside.

"Ah, hello. I am calling from the National Federation of Hip Patients," Grandpa said in a frightfully high-pitched voice. "We were wondering if you would be generous enough to consider purchasing some fundraising scratch cards."

While he was speaking, he pointed desperately at the window. Auntie Granny clearly didn't want any scratch cards, so we didn't have much time.

"Psst! Krølla!" I whispered, letting out the fishing line.

Krølla didn't understand straight away that she had to attach waffles to the hook. She is so little, after all. It took us quite a while to explain, but we managed to hoist up two waffles before Grandpa had to hang up and Auntie Granny came back outside. Lena wolfed one of them down as soon as we got it over the window ledge.

"We've got to share!" I said, almost shouting.

"It's impossible to share two waffles between three people, Trille!" Lena explained with her mouth full.

Grandpa and I had to make do with one. In the garden, Krølla was on her fifth.

After ten minutes, Grandpa fixed a pillowcase

to the end of a broom and raised the white flag out
of the bedroom window. We surrendered.

It's fun to play war. But peace is best. That's what
I thought when I was finally sitting in the garden
eating waffles with the world's nicest granny-aunt.

"Why is he so thin and you're so fat, if you're
brother and sister?" Lena asked, mid-bite, looking
at Auntie Granny and Grandpa.

"She ate all my food when we were little," said
Grandpa, who had to duck as Auntie Granny tried
to smack him with her tea towel.

"I wasn't this fat in the old days, little Lena."

"Exactly how fat were you then?" Lena wanted
to know.

And so the story-telling began. She had been
beautiful, my Auntie Granny, like an actress. There
were so many young men who wanted to marry
her that Grandpa was allowed to lie on the roof and

shoot them with his catapult when they came to see her. Nobody was fat back then, actually, as far as Grandpa could remember, because they only ate potatoes and fish. But at Christmas they were given an orange. Except during the war. They weren't given any then…

Just as we were going to bed, Mum called to see how things were going. Grandpa told her that both young and old were on their best behaviour.

"We've been telling stories about the old days and eating waffles," he said.

Lena and I smiled.

"Can I have a word with Krølla?" Mum asked next.

Grandpa gave a little cough and reluctantly handed over the receiver.

"Don't tell her we've been on the moped," I whispered to Krølla.

She nodded and took the phone with an air of importance.

"What have you been doing today, Little Miss Krølla?" we heard Mum ask.

Grandpa fell to his knees in front of his youngest grandchild and clasped his hands. Krølla looked at him in astonishment.

"I haven't ridden on the moped," she said loud and clearly.

Grandpa dropped his hands, breathing a sigh of relief. Up there at the choral festival, Mum probably did the same thing.

"That's good," she said softly. "What *did* you do then, my sweet?"

"I rode in the box," said Krølla.

CHAPTER SEVEN
Isak

Lena has her birthday once a year, just like everyone else, but you would think it was more often. She talks about her birthday constantly. Now it was finally getting closer.

"It's pretty good turning nine on the ninth of July, isn't it?" she said, pleased.

Her mother had come home from the choral festival and was drying some fruit to make art out of. Lena and I were eating.

"Yes, pretty good. What would you like to get?" her mum said.

"A dad."

Lena's mother sighed and asked if Lena wanted him wrapped or as a gift voucher. "Wouldn't you like something else, Lena love?"

No, Lena didn't want anything else, but even so, when we went out onto the steps she stood still for a moment. Eventually she opened the door a crack and shouted back inside:

"A bike!"

Lena invited all of our class to her birthday party. Eight boys, plus me. A few hours before the party, I went over to check if they'd made enough cake for all the guests. Lena's mum opened the door.

"You've come at just the right time, Trille. Maybe you'll be able to cheer her up."

I went inside, puzzled.

Lena was lying on the sofa. She didn't look well.

"Are you ill?" I asked in dismay.

"Yes, I'm ill! I've got spots on my tummy!" she shouted, almost as if it were my fault. "And nobody wants to come to my party and catch it, because it's the middle of the holidays!"

Lena threw her pillow at the wall, making all the pictures in the living room wobble.

What a disaster.

"Oh, Lena," I said sadly.

After a while, my mum came over to see if I was getting in the way of the cake decorating.

"Goodness me, Lena, are you ill?" she asked, sitting down on the edge of the sofa. Mum knows all about illnesses, having so many children.

"What do you think it is, Kari?" Lena's mum asked as she brought in some tea.

Mum thought it was chickenpox. I'd had chickenpox when I was three, she said, and as it's not possible to get it more than once, I could go to Lena's party after all. If Lena had the energy.

Lena had the energy, and at six o'clock I showed up with her present, wearing my smart shorts. Her present was a croquet set. I think Lena liked it. Croquet mallets can be used for so many things, she said. It was a good party. Lena's mum had set up a bed in the living room, and Lena sat in it giving orders like a queen. We watched DVDs and had the whole cream birthday cake to ourselves. Lena only got angry about her stupid chickenpox once, throwing a cinnamon bun at the wall.

"You've got quite an arm on you," her mother said with a sigh.

Later in the evening, the birthday girl got worse and I thought it would be best to go home. But Lena wasn't having any of that.

"Smoking haddocks," she said, "it wouldn't be

right if the only guest left at half past seven when the party's supposed to last until nine."

I took another piece of cake, while Lena fell asleep.

"I've spoken to them at the surgery," Lena's mum whispered to me. "The on-call doctor is already visiting this side of the fjord this evening, so he'll pop by."

Just then there was a knock at the door. I craned my neck and peeped out into the corridor. The doctor was younger than they usually are, and he looked very nice. The grown-ups stood there for quite a while saying hello and smiling, and as the doctor came into the living room he turned round and smiled back at Lena's mum, causing him to stumble against the door, almost tripping.

"Are you the one who's ill?" he asked me when he'd recovered his balance.

"No, I've had it before," I said proudly, and pointed at Lena over in her bed. If I hadn't done that, I think the doctor would have sat on top of her, and that would have caused quite a fuss! He sat down next to her instead and carefully put his hand on her shoulder. Lena came round slowly at first, and then woke up like a shot. She looked at the doctor as if he'd dropped out of the sky, rubbed her eyes and looked at him some more. Then she jumped up, beaming, and shouted:

"A dad!"

The bit of cake I had on my spoon fell onto my plate.

"But, Mum, you already gave me a bike!" Lena continued, laughing with joy in spite of her spots and fever and everything else.

"I—I'm a doctor," stammered the poor GP.

"Mum, he's a doctor, too! Isn't that handy?"

Lena's mum came running from the kitchen.

"Lena, he's *just* a doctor," I explained, worried that I was going to laugh. There was nothing I could do about it, so I just let it come out, even though Lena might have been incensed. But she was probably so worn out with fever and chickenpox that she didn't have the strength to get angry. She just pulled her blanket over her head and fell back down on the sofa like a sack of potatoes.

When the doctor had finished looking at Lena's chickenpox, there was over an hour until the next ferry left, so Lena invited him to stay for her party. He was called Isak and told us that he'd only just begun to work as a doctor, and that he was worried about getting illnesses wrong or things like that.

"But I do have chickenpox, don't I?" asked Lena.

Yes, Isak was sure about that. Lena definitely had chickenpox.

When he was leaving, Isak saw the motorbike in the utility room. We found out that he also had a motorbike, and the grown-ups ended up standing there talking about motorbikes for so long that he almost missed the ferry.

"That was a pretty good party," said Lena happily, when Isak had finally gone.

Her mother gave a strange smile and nodded.

CHAPTER EIGHT
Christmas carols in the middle of summer

Lena soon got better. And when she got out of bed, she'd decided to become a goalkeeper. She'd been watching football on TV while she was ill.

"It's the keeper who makes the decisions, Trille. He calls out to all the others, telling them where to run."

In that case, I thought Lena was well cut out to be the goalie. She's the only girl in our football team and gets as angry as a hornet over nothing. The other boys in the team often make her angry on purpose, and Lena says that she plays on a team of complete and utter idiots.

In the summer there are no training sessions or matches, but we still play a lot of football, Lena and I, especially when the fields are freshly cut. But we had just lost the ball again. I couldn't find it anywhere. In the end I had to ask Mum if I could have a new one.

"No, Trille. This is the second ball you've lost this year. It's out of the question."

"But I need a ball, Mum!" I said.

"Then you'll have to buy your own, Trille dear."

Grown-ups always say things like that without realizing that it's not so easy for those of us who don't have any money.

Magnus was sitting in the hammock, playing on his mobile. Magnus always has money. Every day during the summer, he and a friend take their guitars to town, where they busk in the pedestrian precinct and people throw money into a hat in front of their feet. I watched him and made a decision. I was going to go into town as well. But Lena would have to come too.

"You think we should sing in the middle of the main street, where everyone will hear us?" she asked when I went in and told her about my plan. She'd made her Special Lena Breakfast, which is so unhealthy that it can only be made when you're at home by yourself.

"We'll have to play instruments," she said in between munches. "Otherwise nobody's going to throw us money."

"But we can only play the recorder," I said.

"Recorders will do fine," Lena said firmly.

And so that was that.

* * *

Now we had to practise. It was so long since we'd rehearsed on our recorders that we'd almost forgotten we had them. We began in our kitchen, but, after a while, Mum said she had to listen to something really important on the radio and asked us to go elsewhere. In the living room we only played one note each before Dad explained that it was very nice, but his head couldn't take such loud noises on Thursdays. Then we went downstairs to Grandpa, but his hearing aid began to whistle, so we had to find somewhere else. In the end we went out into the hay barn and sat on the old tractor.

We practised and practised, but there was only one song we could both manage: "Silent Night". We'd played it at the Christmas concert at school.

"Ooh, I'm getting goose bumps!" said Lena, who thought our playing was a thing of heavenly beauty.

*   *   *

The next morning it was hot with brilliant sunshine and the sea lay stretched out like a light blue sheet. Grandpa's boat was a little dot in the distance. Lena and I ran all the way to the ferry landing, where we waited ten minutes for the ferry. We hid our recorders under our T-shirts as we got on board, but Dad still saw them. He drummed his fingers on his ticket bag and looked sternly at us.

"I don't want to hear a single note while you're on the ferry. The captain might get distracted and crash into the jetty," he said.

We promised. And Dad didn't ask any more.

I'm very fond of our ferry. There's a slot machine on board that Minda knows how to win on and Lena knows how to lose on, a staircase with a railing you can slide down and a kiosk that sells big traditional pancakes with butter and sugar. Margot makes them. Margot is old and can pull toad faces if you ask her enough times.

Lena and I are friends with Margot. We mostly sit with her when we visit Dad at work, but now and then we run up to the top deck and spit in the sea, and sometimes we get to go on the bridge, if they're in the right mood up there.

This time we hurried straight down to Margot.

"Well, if it isn't young Trille, and Lena! Bless you, I haven't seen you all summer!" she said.

"But you must have heard about us," said Lena.

It was true. Margot had heard all sorts of things, about shark boats and manure, she told us.

"You mustn't believe everything you hear," said Lena at that point.

Dad didn't want us to go into town alone, but we badgered him. Magnus was there, and we knew where he went busking. We could even see him from the ferry! Dad gave in eventually. If we promised to stay with Magnus the whole time, we could stay in town and catch the next ferry, but we would have to go right back down to the dock. We promised. Then we ran up the pedestrianized street to Magnus. He and his friend Hassan were in the middle of a song and didn't spot us until they'd finished.

"What are you doing here?" Magnus asked, not entirely happy to see us.

"We're going to earn money for a new football," I said, showing him my recorder.

Magnus and Hassan looked at each other and began to laugh. I could almost feel Lena's temper rising.

"Yes, we are, you'll see!" she shouted at them. "And we have to stay here with you, unfortunately, because Trille's dad said so!"

Before anyone could do anything else, she pulled me up onto a bench close by, took off my cap and threw it down in front of us.

"Come on, Trille!"

I'd forgotten how many people there usually are on a busy shopping street. I felt like I was going to pass out there and then.

"Lena, I'm not really sure I want to do this after all," I whispered without moving my lips.

"Do you want a football or don't you?"

"I do…"

"Play then, for crying out loud!"

My knees shook. My best friend counted to three. And there we stood, on a bench in the middle of the street, playing "Silent Night". Lena got goose bumps from it. I just looked at my recorder. Nobody clapped when we'd finished. People just walked on by.

"One more time," Lena ordered mercilessly.

And so we played one more time. People were very hot and busy, it seemed. But suddenly a lady took hold of her husband's hand and said:

"Gosh, look, Rolf, aren't they sweet?"

She meant Lena and me. We played again and then the lady and her husband named Rolf left twenty kroner in my cap. After that, more than seventeen people stopped at once, all wanting to hear our Christmas carol. Once more I felt a bit like I was going to collapse, but I closed my eyes and thought of the football. Everyone was clapping and laughing and shouting, "Encore, encore!" A crowd had gathered around the bench. Lena and I were almost like pop stars. There was even a lady taking photos, who asked what our names were. Lena gave a deep bow every time we finished playing. And I bowed both to the right and to the left, like Dad does when he conducts the mixed choir.

"We must have enough now," I said eventually.

My hands were all sweaty. Lena peered into the cap and nodded. We said goodbye and climbed down. The cap was heavy with coins. We smiled smugly at Magnus and Hassan and ran up the road to the sports shop next to the council offices. We'd completely forgotten about Dad.

"You're forty-two kroner short," said the man behind the counter once he had checked our money.

His hair was all over the place and looked really stiff. His lip was sticking right out too. I could see Lena leaning forward, wanting to know what he had under it. He was a grumpy man.

"Pff, we can make forty-two kroner quicker than you can say 'stinky trainers'," Lena said.

We set up on the steps outside the sports shop. There weren't as many people there as in the main street, but we kept on playing. Eventually we could play "Silent Night" in nineteen seconds.

After a while, the grumpy man came outside.

"Stop that din! It's scaring my customers away!"

"We can't stop. We still need..." Lena looked at me.

"... twenty-seven kroner," I said.

The man rolled his eyes. Then he stuck his finger under his lip and pulled out a big glob of *snus*, a kind of tobacco that's sucked instead of smoked. He flung it down in front of our feet and slammed the door as he went back in.

"He could do with a trip to the head teacher's office," Lena said strictly, and then we began to play again.

We only got halfway through before the shop door reopened, and the grumpy man shouted, "Put a sock in it! You can have your ball, you wretched children!"

We were standing outside the shop with our new football when I remembered about Dad.

"Oh no!" I shouted, and we started running. The ferry had made three journeys, and Dad was more or less as angry as I had feared. He somehow gets all big and red when he's angry.

"We'll never do it again," I promised, all out of breath.

"Huh! Never do it again indeed! You and Lena never do the same thing twice. You only come up with more madness!"

Lena looked at him kindly and took his hand.

"Have you seen our ball?" she asked. "It's a professional one."

I saw that Dad was starting to look slightly proud of us. He thought it was a nice ball and wanted to try it. But it's not easy to do tricks wearing a ticket bag and wooden shoes. All of a sudden, both his shoe and the ball flew in a beautiful curve overboard. I slapped my forehead. There we'd been, playing "Silent Night" almost to death, and Dad had sent the ball flying into the sea before we'd even had a chance to try it!

"Well, now you'll have to dive into the sea and get it!" Lena shouted angrily.

Dad didn't really fancy diving into the sea. Instead, he ran up onto the jetty and borrowed a net from a German man who was fishing there and managed to lift the ball ashore. His shoe disappeared out to sea.

When Dad had sold tickets to all the passengers, he came down to Margot's kiosk, where Lena and I were.

"Let's not tell Mum that you and Lena have been into town by yourselves today, OK, Trille?"

I promised.

But that didn't help much. The next day there was a big picture of Lena and me in the newspaper. The lady who had been taking photos of us was a journalist.

"You're a sneaky one, you are, Trille, my lad," said Mum, peering up from behind the newspaper.

I promised to play "Silent Night" for her one day when I had time.

CHAPTER NINE
When I whacked Lena on the head

All sorts of strange things happen when you've got a neighbour and best friend like Lena, but sometimes I think I like normal days best of all. Those days when nothing special happens, and I eat liver paste on bread and Lena and I have a kickabout or look for crabs and talk about ordinary things, without anything going wrong.

"Do you think ordinary days are better than Christmas?" asked Lena when I tried to explain what I thought.

"No, but it can't be Christmas every day," I said. "Otherwise Christmas would become boring."

Lena assured me that it could be Christmas much more often without her getting bored in the slightest, and then we said no more about it. We played football out in the sun instead, and while I tried to score against Lena, I thought that this was a nice and ordinary day.

"I ought to have a dad to play football with. One who does really hard kicks," said Lena, after she had saved one of my best shots.

I sighed.

We took a break on the lawn, and Minda, who was painting the balcony, came and sat down with us. Lena and I smiled. Minda is almost as good as Auntie Granny at telling stories and making us feel warm and cosy. She lay down on her stomach and told us why our cove is called Mathildewick.

"The reason is," she said, "that there was once

a Portuguese pirate ship sailing out in the fjord here, and the prow of the ship was mounted with a magnificent figurehead: the beautiful Maid Mathilde."

"A figurehead?" I asked. Minda explained that a figurehead is a big wooden dummy with flowing hair and a beautiful dress that used to be attached to boats in the old days.

"Then came a hurricane, just out there," Minda continued. "A proper, deadly hurricane, like they used to have in the old days. The ship tilted from one side to the other, making it impossible to steer, and eventually the whole thing came crashing into our cove. The beautiful Mathilde whacked into the rocks by the shore, sending splinters flying – more or less where we traditionally put out bonfires using the muck-spreader."

"Wow," Lena and I said, almost in chorus.

"The pirates never got home. They found

themselves wives and settled here instead. And they called the cove Mathildewick after the destroyed figurehead of Mathilde that had whacked into the rocks on the beach." Minda leant towards us and whispered, "One of them was Grandpa's great-great-great-great-grandfather. It's hardly surprising that he's got pirate blood in his veins!"

I was speechless for a long while, thinking that, if this was true, it would be fantastic.

"Minda," I said at last, "does that mean I have pirate blood in my veins too then?"

"You've all got pirate blood in you; the whole family apart from me, because I'm an adopted Inca princess." She laughed. Then she walked on her hands all the way back up to the house to continue painting the balcony.

Lena took the football and threw it up into the air a couple of times while I sat there, almost feeling like I was a different boy from the one

I had been a short while ago. I had pirate blood in my veins.

"Maybe that's why I do so many crazy things. I can't help it. I'm full of pirate blood," I said to Lena.

"Bah! You've got so little of it that it all runs out of you if you so much as get a nosebleed," she said sharply.

Lena was probably thinking she wouldn't mind having some pirate blood of her own.

I looked out over the sea. There was Grandpa in his boat. Naturally! He was a pirate!

"Lena, why don't we go out in the rubber dinghy?" I suggested. The pirate blood in me wanted to go to sea too.

Lena gave me a resigned look but took off her goalkeeping gloves.

"OK. Bagsy I get to be that Mathilde who got whacked on the rocks!"

*　　*　　*

When Lena came aboard my bright yellow rubber dinghy a little later, she was wearing her mother's long red dress under her lifejacket and had a majestic look on her face. I doubted that she was supposed to go to sea in a dress like that, but so be it.

We rowed around the jetty. I felt like a pirate and was happy and contented, but Lena, who was hanging over the prow, quickly began to feel it was boring being a figurehead.

"Here comes the storm," she announced.

I began to rock backwards and forwards, making Lena's hair skim the sea below. She remained as still as a chest of drawers. Eventually she turned round and said impatiently, "Are you going to whack me on the head soon or not?"

I shrugged my shoulders and rowed carefully towards the jetty. The dinghy drifted slowly forwards. But, at that very moment, Grandpa arrived on his boat. He made large waves, and one of them gave the rubber dinghy such a shove that we smacked into the concrete with a crack.

Rubber dinghies don't go *crack*. Figureheads, on the other hand, make a tremendous crack. Especially their heads.

"Lena!" I screamed when I saw her hanging lifelessly over the prow. "Grandpa, Lena's dead!"

Grandpa came as quickly as he could and pulled Lena out of the dinghy. "Hey, come on, little lass, wake up," he said, shaking her gently.

I sat holding the oars, not knowing what to do. I just cried.

"Uh…" groaned Lena. She opened her eyes and looked at Grandpa as if she didn't recognize him. Then she groaned some more.

"There, there," said Grandpa. "Let's get you to the doctor. And you, Trille, my lad, you can stop crying. She's OK."

Lena half stood up. "No, just keep on crying, Trille, you smoked haddock! You row like an idiot!"

I have never been so happy to hear someone say something so mean to me. Lena was all right; she'd only got a medium whack to her head.

But then Lena realized her forehead was bleeding and she let out a furious scream. She had to go into town to see the doctor and, as I waved her goodbye, I thought to myself that there isn't really any such thing as an ordinary day when you've got a neighbour and best friend like Lena.

CHAPTER TEN
Summer's end

Grandpa usually gets up before the early bird farts in the bush, as he says. Sometimes, in summer, I do too. Then I run for all I'm worth down to the sea. Often Grandpa's already gone, and I can see him far out at sea like a little dot. That's one of the saddest things I know, standing on the jetty with just the seagulls for company early in the morning, though not early enough. But sometimes I manage to catch him.

"Well, if it isn't my young lad Trille!" Grandpa says then, delighted.

That's what's so great about Grandpa. I know that he's as fond of me as I am of him. With Lena it's so difficult to know.

That day I made it in time. Before it turned six, we were far out at sea, Grandpa and I. We drew in the nets and didn't say anything much. It was good to have him all to myself.

"Minda says we're part pirate," I said, after looking at him for a while.

Grandpa stood up straight, and I told him the whole story about Mathildewick. When I'd finished, he laughed loudly.

"Isn't it true?" I asked, beginning to smell a rat.

"That Little Miss Minda, she tells such good lies it's like music to my ears," said Grandpa, impressed. "We could all learn something from her."

"Auntie Granny says that people shouldn't tell lies," I said.

"Mm-hmm," said Grandpa, still laughing to himself. "Was that why you ran Lena into the jetty yesterday, then?" he asked.

I nodded and thought about Lena, who had come home with a bandage over her forehead the previous evening. It was Isak who had patched her up. She was pleased about that. What was worse was that she had minor concussion and would have to take it easy for a whole week.

"Uh-oh," Mum had said when she found out.

The last time Lena had concussion, everyone in Mathildewick Cove almost went mad. Lena isn't good at taking it easy.

As Grandpa and I approached the shore, I could see Lena standing at the end of the jetty like a small, slender statue.

"Fishing, fishing, fishing!" she said flatly as we bumped into the jetty. She was in such a bad mood that the sky darkened above where she stood.

Poor Lena. I wanted to say something that would make her happy, so I told her that I wasn't a pirate after all and that Minda had made the whole thing up.

"I got whacked for nothing!" Lena howled, stamping her foot and sending pebbles flying everywhere.

I soon saw that it was more than Lena's concussion that was making her angry.

"Look," she said, thrusting a brochure at Grandpa's stomach. "I went to get the post, thinking I might get a card or something, being poorly and so on, and then there's this advert for school bags instead!"

I looked at the brochure. BACK TO SCHOOL, it said. Lena is so fond of the summer holidays. She doesn't like school at all.

"I'm going to hibernate," she moaned, "and sleep until next summer."

We felt sorry for Lena. Nobody said a word as we began to stroll up towards the farm with the fish tub between us.

"You're so lucky not having to go to school," Lena mumbled to Grandpa when we got back to the house and were standing under the balcony. Grandpa stepped out of his wooden shoes and opened his door. Yes, he agreed with Lena, he was incredibly lucky, and he would have liked to make us waffles to cheer us up. "But it'll have to be fresh fish and new potatoes instead," he said.

"I know ... because you don't know how to make waffles," sulked Lena, with her concussion.

"In actual fact, our cove isn't called Mathildewick," Grandpa told us as he was cooking. "We just call it that because years ago a lady called

Mathilde lived here. She had fourteen children and a husband who was called Viktor, or Vik, so they called her Mathilde Vik, like they call me Lars Yttergård after the old name of our farm, which has become our surname too."

"So was our cove called Mathildewick just because of that?" I asked.

Grandpa nodded.

"You can't invent a game with that," I said, disappointed.

"No, luckily not!" exclaimed Lena.

After we'd eaten, Lena and I climbed up into the cedar tree and sat there without saying anything. I could feel the summer running away from me as I looked at our cove through the branches. It was as if everything had changed slightly. The fields weren't as green any more and the wind wasn't as warm. Lena sighed one of her Maths lesson sighs.

"Ah, it's rubbish how time flies," she said eventually.

The following week, Lena and I began our fourth year at school, as in Norway we start at six years old. I thought it was good to be back, even if I didn't say so to Lena. We had a new teacher called Ellisiv. She was young and had a big smile. I liked her straight away.

What was not so good was that Kai-Tommy was still just as nasty and teased the rest of us as much as before the holidays. He's the one who's really in charge in our class. He thought our class would be perfect if Lena wasn't in it, because then there would be only boys. Lena usually gets so angry when he says things like that that she snarls at him, but this autumn she had a good comeback:

"Smoking haddocks! We've got Ellisiv, you circus llama! She's a girl, isn't she?"

I realized that Lena liked our new teacher, even if she had sat looking sternly at Ellisiv for the first four days without answering a single question.

"Lena's very nice when you get used to her," I told Ellisiv when I was last out of the classroom one day. I was afraid she might get completely the wrong end of the stick about her.

"I think both you and Lena are very nice. Are you best friends?" Ellisiv asked.

I took a step closer. "One half of us is," I whispered.

Ellisiv thought that was a promising start to a best friendship.

Then football training started. What a drama that was. Lena said that she was now the goalkeeper for our team. Kai-Tommy said that was the stupidest thing he'd heard since he last saw Lena. We couldn't have a girl in goal! Lena became so angry that the mountains trembled, and our coach let her have a trial for one session. She jumped around in goal like a frog. Nobody managed to score. So Lena became our goalie, and one weekend, in town, we won the local cup tournament thanks to her. Lena was as proud as a peahen.

I told Auntie Granny about the cup when I spoke to her on the phone. But she doesn't care about football in the slightest. She thinks it's a load of nonsense.

"There's an old lady here with a waffle iron that's been cold for several weeks," she complained. "Can't you two put away that ball and come to visit me instead?"

We were happy to. I asked Dad straight away, and he said that would be fine, as he was going to pick up Auntie Granny that weekend to bring her round to our house.

*　　*　　*

It's about twelve miles to Auntie Granny's. Dad was driving, and Lena felt sick, but she didn't throw up. She just looked very pale.

Auntie Granny lives alone in a small, yellow house surrounded by roses. Dad has asked her many times whether she would like to move in with us in Mathildewick Cove instead. I have asked her too. But Auntie Granny doesn't want to. She's perfectly happy in her yellow house.

We stayed at Auntie Granny's all afternoon and helped with her chores. The sky had darkened and it had started to rain when we went in. Auntie Granny had set the table, and everything was so cosy and welcoming that I had a lump in my throat. Sitting indoors on Auntie Granny's sofa and eating waffles when it's raining outside is the best thing in the world. I tried to think of something better, but couldn't come up with anything.

While we were eating, Lena tried to teach Auntie Granny about football.

"It's important to shoot hard, really hard!" she explained.

"Oh dear," said Auntie Granny.

"Was there a lot of shooting here during the war?" I asked, because Auntie Granny much prefers talking about the war than about football.

"No, Trille, my laddie, luckily not, but there were many other things that weren't very pleasant."

And then Auntie Granny told us that people weren't allowed to have radios during the war, because the German soldiers were afraid the Norwegians would cheer each other up with their radio programmes.

"But we had a radio all the same," she smiled slyly. "We buried it behind the hay barn, and then we dug it out when we wanted to listen to it."

Auntie Granny and Grandpa's parents did a lot of illegal things during the war, because when there's an invasion, everything's turned inside out: illegal things actually become the most right thing to do.

"I wish it was like that normally," Lena said, but Auntie Granny said that we shouldn't wish for that. It was very dangerous in case you were found out. If anyone had known that her father listened to the radio, they would have sent him away.

"Then you wouldn't have had a dad either," said Lena.

"No, you're quite right," said Auntie Granny, stroking Lena's head.

"Where did they send people who listened to the radio, then?" I asked.

"To a camp," said Auntie Granny.

"With tents and caravans?" asked Lena, confused.

"No, to a concentration camp. The one in Norway was called Grini. And it was a terrible place," Auntie Granny explained.

Lena looked at her thoughtfully for a while. "How scared were you?" she asked in the end.

"Auntie Granny is never scared," I said, before she had a chance to answer. "She has Jesus above her head when she sleeps." I took Lena through to Auntie Granny's bedroom to show her.

"There," I said, pointing to a picture above her bed. In it there's a steep rock face with a little lamb standing on a narrow ledge, unable to get up or down. The mother ewe is standing at the top, bleating, very afraid for her lamb. But Jesus is there too, and he fastens his staff to a tree and leans out over the cliff edge to rescue the lamb.

Lena tilted her head and looked at the picture for a long time. "Is it magic?" she asked eventually.

I didn't know. I only knew that Auntie Granny is

never afraid, because she has Jesus above her bed. She says that all people are like little lambs and that Jesus looks after them.

When we went home, I got to sit in the front and help change the gears. Lena sat in the back with Auntie Granny. She felt more and more sick, and when we were almost home, she threw up copiously on a tuft of red clovers.

"It's because you change the gears like an idiot, Trille," said my best friend in a car-sick voice once she'd scrambled back into the car. I acted as if I hadn't heard. It probably didn't help that Lena had eaten nine waffles with butter and sugar.

"You'd better get well for tomorrow, missy!" said Dad when we finally got home. "Then you'll be ready to round up the sheep."

Both Lena and I opened our eyes wide.

"Are *we* getting to help?" I almost shouted.

"Yes, I think you must be old enough now," Dad said in a completely normal voice.

I couldn't believe that anyone could be so happy!

CHAPTER ELEVEN

*Rounding up the sheep –
and a helicopter ride*

*A*ll summer, our sheep wander around up
on the mountain doing whatever they like.
But before winter comes, we have to head up there
and bring them back down to the barn.

"That's their holidays finally over too, the lucky
cods," Lena usually says. She thinks it's unfair that
sheep get longer summer holidays than people.

This time Lena and I were going to help!
I almost couldn't believe it when we were standing

outside on the decking the next day. My whole family were there, minus Krølla. So were Lena and her mum, and Uncle Tor. Dad, wearing his rucksack and his cap, asked if everyone was ready. As we set off up the slopes, Lena and I were able to wave to Grandpa and Auntie Granny and Krølla, instead of standing down there waving up, as we had always done before. Although Lena had never waved up at anyone. She always sat with her back turned when the others went to round up the sheep, as sour as an unripe stalk of rhubarb.

It definitely wasn't summer any more. The air was sharp and the trees above our heads hung heavy with dew as we passed Hillside Jon's farm and entered the spruce forest. Lena and I were wearing our wellies, and we jumped in all the puddles we found along the path, like two rabbits.

"You should walk at a steady pace," said Dad. "Otherwise you'll just get tired."

But how could we walk at a steady pace when we were that excited? Our feet ran by themselves!

We soon came out of the forest and up onto the mountain itself. It's almost flat there and everything looks different.

"It's because we're closer to the sky," said Lena's mum, jumping from stone to stone with Lena and me. When we turned round, we saw our cove far, far below us. Now and then we spotted sheep. Sometimes they were ours, and sometimes they were other people's. But we weren't rounding them up today. First we were going to stay a night in the cabin.

Our cabin is really just a hut, without any electricity and without a toilet. But there's space for lots of people if they sleep head to toe. I think it's the best cabin in the world. It reminds me of Auntie Granny, because it seems so happy when we arrive. Soon there were mountain smells surrounding us on all sides. Mum and Uncle Tor were frying bacon on the gas stove inside, and outside Dad was making coffee on the bonfire.

Dad's so happy when he's up on the mountain. Then you can ask him about things that you wouldn't normally dare to ask about, and he laughs almost the whole time.

"You can't be angry up on the mountain," he explained when I told him. "Do you know what I mean, Trille?"

I searched my feelings and nodded. Lena thought if that's the way things were, then Dad should go up on the mountain much more often. She was sitting on the other side of him, staring into the bonfire. I wished I could have given Lena a bit of my dad right then, so she could feel what it was like to have one – one who makes bonfires and who likes being in the mountains. Actually, she should get to borrow him now and then.

"Yes, every Wednesday afternoon or something," she said when I mentioned it. "Then I could take him up the mountain to give him a walk."

Then came rounding-up day. Lena and I were supposed to go with Uncle Tor over some hilltops called the Peaks. They're flat on one side, but on the other side they go straight down. Dad pointed and explained. He's been rounding up sheep every year since he was the same age as me.

"Take good care of the children!" he told his younger brother.

"Aye, aye," answered Uncle Tor.

My uncle is someone who walks in long strides, and Lena and I were only just able to keep up. I think he thought we were too young to be there, and he wanted to prove that he was right.

"You're not exactly taking good care of us!" Lena shouted angrily when she had to stop and empty her welly and Uncle Tor just kept on going.

He didn't hear.

"Come on, Lena," I said.

"No!"

"But we're rounding up the sheep!"

"Yes!"

She stood completely still. I sighed and lowered my hood. And then I heard it too. A weak, frightened bleat that was almost not like bleating at all.

Lena and I followed the sound. It was coming from the edge. We lay down on our stomachs and snaked our way forward.

"Uh-oh," I said.

A ewe was standing on a ledge further down. She must have been there for a long time. She was so weak that she barely had the strength to bleat. Imagine if we hadn't stumbled upon her! I crept even further forward and read her ear tag. The yellow clip said 3011.

"She's ours."

"I wonder how she got down there," Lena said, crawling even further forward.

"Over there, most likely," I said, pointing at a small, steep crevice that went down to the ledge. I got up and looked across the Peaks for Uncle Tor. He had vanished. When I turned back towards Lena, she had vanished too.

My heart began thumping so hard that it hurt.

"Lena," I whispered.

No answer.

"Lena!"

"Over here!"

In astonishment, I peered over the edge.

"Who do I look like now?" she shouted, looking at me excitedly from down below. She was hanging from a mountain birch in the crevice, her yellow wellies resting against some tufts of grass on a little outcrop in the rock wall.

"Yourself."

Lena rolled her eyes and reached even further into the air with her free hand, as if she were trying to get hold of the sheep far down below.

"I look like that Jesus, can't you see?"

I tilted my head.

"Jesus didn't have a red rain jacket. Come back up here."

So then Lena tried to take off her rain jacket while hanging there.

"Lena, come back up here!" I shouted, frightened, edging my way forward so she could grasp my hand.

But as Lena took a step upwards, the birch came loose from the rock face and, with the tree in her hand and a scream from her mouth, she disappeared.

Lena has fallen down from high places quite a few times during my life, but I'd never been so scared that she was dead as I was then. I'll never forget the terrible feeling I had in my stomach as I pulled myself as far towards the edge as I dared and peered down the very steep mountainside.

"Ow! My hand!" came a moan from far, far below. My best friend was sitting on a ledge just below the sheep, rocking back and forth. I was so relieved that I could have cried.

"Oh, Lena."

"Oh, Lena, oh, Lena! I've broken my hand!" she shouted, furious.

I could see that she was really hurt. But Lena never cries. Not even then.

If only I could tell you how fast I ran that day! I was terrified that Lena would get bored of sitting on her rock ledge and start climbing. That would have been just like her. I ran so fast that my mouth tasted of blood, and the whole time

I pictured Lena, in her red rain jacket, in free fall, like an angry little superwoman. I realized, suddenly, that if anything happened to Lena, I wouldn't be able to bear it. Where was Uncle Tor? Who would have thought an uncle could walk so far without looking back one single time? I shouted and ran and fell and shouted again. And ran. All the way to the last of the Peaks, where it starts to flatten out. I finally found my uncle there, and by then I was so frightened and angry that I just screamed.

"I should tumble down from the Peaks more often if they give you a helicopter ride every time," Lena said when we were sitting in the cedar tree a couple of days later.

She was excited about everything that had happened – most of all because she had been winched up by a helicopter.

"Then Mum and Isak and I went to a café, after I'd had the cast put on. I've been to the doctor's so many times that it called for a celebration, they said." Lena laughed and tapped her plaster cast. "Don't you wish you'd fallen down from the Peaks too, Trille?"

I smiled, but didn't say anything. I don't think Lena realized how scared I'd been. I wasn't able to tell her either. But when I went to bed at night, I couldn't help thinking a slightly sad thought: Lena definitely wouldn't have been as worried about me if I'd been sitting on that ledge.

CHAPTER TWELVE
Lena lashes out

One day Isak suddenly came to visit when nobody was ill. He turned into the farmyard on his motorbike while Lena and I were playing croquet. Lena was so stunned that she hit the ball into the hedge. I could tell she was really annoyed – she hates losing.

"There's nothing wrong with me," she told Isak gruffly.

Isak thought it was good that nothing was wrong with Lena. It was unusual, he said, but very good. And then he told us that he'd brought a part for the half-finished motorbike in the utility room.

"Mum's not home yet. Did she order it?" Lena asked him sceptically.

"No, it's a surprise," said Isak.

He looked a little nervous and embarrassed. I imagined I would have been the same if I'd come on a surprise visit and the first thing I'd seen was Lena with a croquet mallet.

"Why don't you play with us until she comes back?" I blurted out before Lena could say anything else.

Isak was glad to join us. Lena fell completely silent for a moment, but then I saw that she'd found the ball in the hedge.

"Ha, now we've got to start again," she mumbled in satisfaction as she picked it up.

* * *

Isak began to visit more often. The half-finished motorbike at Lena's gradually started to look like a finished one. Lena didn't say anything about their visitor for the first few weeks. It was as if she were pretending that Isak didn't exist.

But then one day, when we were sitting in the cedar tree watching him and her mother putting spruce branches in the flowerbeds, Lena said:

"He doesn't like boiled cabbage."

I leant forward so I could see through the branches better.

"Does it really matter that much about the cabbage, Lena?"

Lena shrugged. I could see that she was thinking carefully.

"But what use are they otherwise, Trille?"

I couldn't come up with anything this time either and felt a bit guilty for Dad.

"My dad eats boiled carrots, too," I said after a

while, just to say something.

So did Isak, a beaming Lena reported the following day. She'd got him to eat three of her carrots in addition to his own. Grandpa laughed and said, "Poor creature." And then Lena ran off again, because that poor creature was still visiting. I watched her disappear through the hole in the hedge.

"I think Lena has more fun with Isak than with me," I said to Grandpa.

Grandpa was sitting there trying to darn a hole in a sock. He looks like an owl when he's wearing his glasses.

"It's good for Lena to have an Isak. *Ouch!* So you'll just have to put up with it, Trille lad."

"Yes," I said, after thinking for a while.

Grandpa's usually right.

I don't know if it was the thing with the carrots that did it, but Lena was so happy then, it was

like having some kind of butterfly as a neighbour.
Things like that are strange when you're not used
to them.

Then suddenly, one Wednesday at the end of
November, she was back to the same old Lena.
But even angrier. I noticed it as soon as we met to
walk to school. She didn't say hi, which is always
a danger sign. It was almost good to see she could
still be like that. It's more normal. I didn't say
anything, though. It wouldn't have been a good
idea. Nobody should say anything to Lena when
she's like that. But Kai-Tommy did. As always.
And this time he regretted it.

It was at breaktime. Most people had finished
eating and were heading outside. Ellisiv was sitting
at her desk, writing. When Lena walked past Kai-
Tommy, he said, so quietly that Ellisiv couldn't hear
it, "Oh, can you imagine what it'd be like if we got
rid of the girls in this class?"

Lena turned around sharply. I felt a tingle begin to go up my spine. The other boys also realized that something was about to happen, because suddenly everyone was looking at Lena and Kai-Tommy. Lena stood there, as thin as a piece of crispbread, with her pigtails out of line, and so angry that I held my breath.

"If you say that one more time, I'm going to thump you all the way to Nerdvika."

Kai-Tommy smiled nastily, leant a little closer and said:

"Oh, can you imagine what it'd be like if we got rid of the girls in this class?"

Then came the blow. Lena Lid, my best friend and neighbour, thumped Kai-Tommy in the middle of his face, sending him flying in an arc up to the desk where Ellisiv was sitting. It was like in a film. Like in a 15, which I'm not allowed to watch but I've seen some anyway.

And it was Lena who did it. She struck him with the hand that had just come out of the plaster cast, dealing a blow that people spoke about for weeks afterwards.

Apart from Kai-Tommy whimpering on the floor, the room was completely silent. We were all in shock – even Ellisiv. I wasn't surprised: a whole pupil had almost landed on her head. But when Lena went towards the door, about to leave the room, our teacher shouted in an angry voice:

"Lena Lid, where do you think you're going?"

Lena turned round and looked at Ellisiv.

"To the head teacher's office," she said.

By the time we shuffled off home that day, Lena had been thoroughly told off, but she hadn't said sorry to Kai-Tommy. She had apologized to the head teacher, she said, and that would just have to do. She had a letter to take home, which she clutched in her sore hand, hidden under her jacket.

"Everyone thinks it's brilliant that you're in our class, Lena. They think you're the toughest and the coolest girl in the whole school. They said so themselves," I told her.

It was true. All the boys had been in awe of Lena that day.

"It doesn't make any difference," Lena said sadly.

"What do you mean?"

Lena didn't answer.

When we got home, Isak was there. That was good, because Lena's hand hurt terribly.

"He's got such a hard face, that Kai-Tommy," she said, giving Isak the letter. He passed it on to Lena's mum.

"Oh, Lena love, what are we going to do with you?" said her mum.

Isak thought Lena had fractured her hand again.

"He must have flown miles, that Kai-Tommy," he said, pretty impressed.

I paced out the distance for Isak on the kitchen floor, adding a couple of paces to be extra kind to Lena.

CHAPTER THIRTEEN
Snow

It's difficult to know when winter is on the way, because it comes so quietly. But when Mum says that I've got to wear my long johns, then it's not long to go. And now the long johns day had come. They felt horrible at first, especially as I was wearing jeans on top. I walked around the house three times to get used to them before I rang Lena's doorbell.

"Have you started wearing your thermals?" I asked.

Lena hadn't. She was going to wait until the snow came.

Going outside to investigate, we saw that it wouldn't be long before Lena would have to put on her long johns too. There was ice on the puddles. And beyond the fjord, God had sprinkled icing sugar on the highest mountain tops.

"I'm looking forward to the snow," I said to Lena.

"It won't be too bad," she replied, not in the best of moods. I couldn't understand what was wrong; Lena usually gets wildly excited about snow. But I didn't want to annoy her. That definitely wouldn't help.

In the afternoon, I got to go with Dad to Auntie Granny's again. Auntie Granny wasn't looking forward to the snow coming, she said, because she can't shovel it away. She's too old. I think I'd like winter even more if I couldn't shovel snow.

It should be allowed to lie there until it disappears by itself. Or until Dad shovels it.

Auntie Granny told stories while Dad and I ate waffles. They were even better than usual, since it was so cold outside. I sat with my legs on the sofa, snuggled up by Auntie Granny, and was so happy that it almost hurt. Auntie Granny has the biggest and warmest heart I know of. There's only one thing wrong with her, and that's her knitting. Especially now Christmas was getting closer.

When Auntie Granny went to the kitchen to fetch more waffles, I had a quick peep into the basket behind the sofa. There was her knitting. In big piles. She always gives us knitted things for Christmas. It's strange that, being as wise as she is, she doesn't understand how awful it is to wear knitted jumpers. They itch, and they look odd. I would much rather have presents from the shops, but Auntie Granny doesn't know about such modern things, even though I've tried to explain it to her a thousand times.

Before we left, I went into her bedroom and looked at the picture of Jesus above her bed. Auntie Granny came in too, and I told her how Lena had been trying to play Jesus when she fell down from the Peaks. As I was telling her, I remembered how scared I had been.

"I'm often scared of losing Lena," I said. "But I don't think she's scared of losing me."

"Maybe Lena knows that she doesn't need to be scared of losing you," said Auntie Granny. "You're such a loyal laddie, Trille."

I searched my feelings, and felt that I was loyal.

"Is it true that you're never scared, Auntie Granny?"

Auntie Granny put her hand on the back of my neck and patted me.

"Maybe I am a little scared sometimes, but then

I just look at that picture and remember that Jesus is taking care of me. You don't need to be scared, Trille, my laddie. It never helps anyone."

"It's a nice picture," I said, and promised to come back when the snow arrived. I could do the shovelling, even though it was boring. Then Auntie Granny gave me a nice, wrinkly Auntie-Granny-hug and promised me a stack of waffles whether I did the shovelling or not.

On Sunday, the snow came.

And on Sunday, Auntie Granny died.

It was Mum who woke me and told me. First she said that it was snowing, and then that Auntie Granny had died. That was the wrong order. It would have been better if she had said that Auntie Granny wasn't alive any more first, and then cheered me up with the snow afterwards. Something inside me fell to pieces. I stayed lying on my pillow while Mum stroked my hair.

It was a strange day. Even Dad and Grandpa cried. That was the worst part. The whole world had been changed, because there was no Auntie Granny any more. And outside it was snowing.

Eventually I put on my snowsuit and went over to the barn, where I lay down. My thoughts flew around like snowflakes, and everything was a mess. Yesterday Auntie Granny had been just as alive as me, and today she was completely dead. What if I died too? It can happen to children. Lena's second cousin died in a road accident. He was only ten. Death is almost like snow; you don't know when it's going to come, even if it tends to come in winter.

Suddenly Lena was there. She was wearing her green snowsuit.

"I've started to wear my thermals. What are you lying here for? You look like a herring."

"Auntie Granny is dead."

"Oh…"

Lena sat down in the snow and went quiet for a moment.

"Was it a cardigan arrest?"

"A cardiac arrest," I answered.

"Oh no," said Lena. "And today when there's snow and everything."

It's often difficult to understand that people are dead, Mum explained that evening. It was warm and safe in her arms. She was right. I wasn't able to understand anything. It was strange that I would never see Auntie Granny again.

"You can see her one last time, if you'd like," said Mum.

I'd never seen a dead person before. But that Tuesday I got to see Auntie Granny. I was dreading it. Lena said that all dead people have blue faces, especially those who have died of heart attacks. I think Magnus and Minda were dreading it too. Krølla just sat up on Dad's shoulders, grinning.

But it wasn't creepy. Auntie Granny wasn't blue. She looked like she was sleeping. I almost thought she was going to open her eyes. Maybe all this dying was only a mistake? I stood there for a long time, watching her eyelids. They didn't move. Imagine if she could open them and look at me and say, "My goodness, Trille, my young laddie, how smart you look!" I had dressed up smart, even if Auntie Granny was dead and couldn't see anything at all. Before we left, I touched her hand. She was cold. Almost like snow.

The funeral was on Thursday, but I'd been to one before. Lena got to come along. She'd known Auntie Granny too. I think Lena thought it was pretty boring at the funeral. I couldn't cry.

"Now Auntie Granny's in heaven," Mum said when we came home.

That was hard to believe, I thought, because they'd buried her coffin down in the earth at the graveyard.

"Is it true, Grandpa?" I asked a little later, "that Auntie Granny's in heaven?"

Grandpa was sitting in his rocking chair, looking straight ahead, wearing his best suit.

"Yes, it's as true as the day is long, Trille lad. The angels will have a good time up there now! And here we are…"

He didn't say any more.

Mathildewick Cove was in mourning now. The whole beginning of December was strange and quiet and full of bouquets of flowers. We missed Auntie Granny. Eventually Lena threw open

our door with a bang and said that I should
come out and throw snowballs, and stop being
a rotten haddock.

"What's wrong with you? You haven't got
concussion, have you?" She stood there impatiently
in her snowsuit.

And so we threw snowballs, Lena and I.
Actually, it was good. Afterwards I wanted to
go over to Lena's, because it had been so long.

"You're not allowed," she said harshly.

I didn't understand, but my neighbour had
a very determined expression on her face, so I
didn't ask any more. Maybe she had an enormous
surprise Christmas present for me in there.

Christmas came that year too, but everything
was different, since Auntie Granny wasn't there
with us. Nobody was sitting at her place at the
table. Nobody folded up the wrapping paper and

said that it was bad to throw away such nice paper. Nobody sang in a high-pitched old lady's voice when we went round the Christmas tree, and it was Mum who had to gather us in front of the Christmas crib and read the Nativity story. And I didn't receive any knitted jumpers. Imagine being sad about that!

In the evening, Lena dropped in to say Merry Christmas. We went up to the ropeway window. I noticed that Lena had closed the curtains in her room. What was it that she didn't want me to see? She'd given me some shin pads for Christmas, so it couldn't be another present. It was almost two weeks since I'd last been to their house.

"Is heaven above the stars?" Lena asked before I had a chance to ask her anything myself.

I peered up and said that I thought it must be. Auntie Granny would be pottering around up there with the angels and Jesus. I expect she'd given them knitted jumpers for Christmas.

"They're probably itching between the wings now," I said. "The angels, I mean."

But Lena didn't feel particularly sorry for the angels.

"They'll be eating waffles too," she said.

Then I remembered what I hadn't told Lena:

"I've inherited something. I was allowed to choose one thing from Auntie Granny's house that would be only for me."

"Were you allowed to choose anything at all?" Lena asked.

I nodded.

"What did you choose, then? The sofa?"

"I chose her picture of Jesus. It's hanging above my bed, so now I don't need to be afraid any more."

Lena went quiet for a long time. I had thought she would tease me for not choosing the sofa or something else big, but she didn't. She just pressed her nose against the windowpane and made a strange face.

CHAPTER FOURTEEN
The saddest day of my life

I thought that now Auntie Granny had died, it would be a long, long time before something sad happened again. But that wasn't the case.

"Are you all right, Trille dear?" Mum asked on the day after Boxing Day. She sat down with me after I'd made a slice of bread with liver paste for dinner.

"Yes," I said, smiling.

"But it's going to be quite lonely for you when Lena leaves, my sweet."

It was like the piece of bread dried up in my mouth.

"Who's leaving?" I asked, breathless.

Mum stared at me. She looked shocked.

"Hasn't Lena told you that she's moving? They've been packing for several weeks!"

I tried to swallow the bread, but it just sat there. Mum took my hand and squeezed it hard.

"My darling Trille! Didn't you know?"

I shook my head. Mum squeezed my hand even harder and, while I sat in silence, she told me that Lena's mum had half a year left to do at art school, which she hadn't finished before Lena was born. Now she'd got back into the school, so they were going to move to town. They were going to live next to Isak. Maybe Lena would have a real dad soon.

I sat there, the bread and liver paste in my mouth, unable to swallow it or spit it out. So that was why I hadn't been let in! Lena was going to move! She was going to go right ahead and move without even saying anything! I could see that Mum was really sorry for me. And I could understand why!

This was not on! I got up so fast that the kitchen chair fell over. I ran out in Magnus's shoes and hit at the hedge as I went through that horrible hole. It was so dark that I tripped on Lena's steps, sending my liver paste and bread down the wrong way. Spluttering and angry, I threw open the door, like Lena usually does, and stomped inside.

There were cardboard boxes everywhere. Lena's mother appeared from behind one of them, surprised. We stood there looking at each other. Suddenly I didn't know what to say. The cardboard boxes were so strange. Lena's house didn't look like itself any more.

Lena sat in the kitchen, not eating her dinner. I went right over to her. I thought I'd yell, like she normally does. I was going to shout – so loud it echoed round the half-empty kitchen – that you can't just move without telling people! I'd opened my mouth to do it – but then it didn't come out. Lena didn't look like herself any more either.

"Are you going to move?" I whispered eventually.

Lena turned round and looked out of the kitchen window. We could see each other's reflection there. We looked at each other in the dark window, and then Lena got up and sneaked her way past me. She disappeared into her room. And closed the door quietly.

Lena's mum dropped everything she was holding.

"Didn't you know, Trille?" she asked, looking even more shocked than Mum. There was a piece of tape stuck in her hair. She climbed over the cardboard boxes and threw her arms around me.

"I'm so sorry! We'll come and visit lots, I promise. It's not far from town."

*   *   *

For the rest of the week, Lena and I each sat in our houses and waited.

"Aren't you going out to play with Lena before she goes?" Mum kept on asking. And I felt that I was the only one in the whole world who understood Lena. Of course we couldn't play now.

On New Year's Eve, we held a farewell party at our house, with loads of food and fireworks. Isak was there too. I couldn't bring myself to speak to him or Lena. Besides, Lena didn't speak to anyone. She sat there looking angry all evening – her mouth set in a straight line. It only turned into a circle when Grandpa stuck one finger in each of her cheeks and pressed so that he could pop in a chocolate.

When the removal lorry came, I stood at the ropeway window, watching the removal men, Lena's mum and Isak carrying the cardboard boxes out of the white house. Lena came last of all. I'd been wondering whether they would have to carry her, too, but she walked by herself and sat down in the back of Isak's car. I felt that I had to go outside, but first I went to my room and took down the picture of Jesus.

Lena didn't look at me. There was a thick car window between us. I knocked, and was a little surprised when she wound it down. To be fair, it was only a small gap, but it was just big enough for me to push Jesus through. And just big enough for me to say Goodbye. But it was apparently too small for Lena to say it.

"Goodbye," I whispered one more time, while Lena gripped my picture and turned away.

Then they drove off.

That evening I was so sad that I didn't know what to do. It was completely impossible to get to sleep.

Dad must have understood, because he came up to my room long after he had said good night. He brought his guitar.

I didn't say anything. Neither did Dad, who sat on the edge of the bed. But after a while, he cleared his throat and began to play. He played the Trille tune, just like when I was tiny. It's my very own song, and it was Dad who wrote it. When he'd finished, he said that he'd written a brand-new song for me, called "Sad Son, Sad Dad".

"Do you want to hear it, Trille?"

I gave a tiny nod.

And as the wintry wind swirled round the house and everyone else slept, my dad played "Sad Son, Sad Dad". I almost couldn't see him because it was so dark. I just listened.

And suddenly I realized what dads are for.

When he'd finished, I cried and cried. Because Lena didn't have a dad, because Auntie Granny was dead and because my best friend had moved away without saying goodbye.

"I never want to get out of bed again!"

That was all right, said Dad, he would take food up to me even if I stayed there right up until my confirmation. Then I cried even more, because it was going to be a terrible life.

"Will I ever be happy again?" I asked.

"Of course you'll be happy again, Trille, my boy," said Dad, lifting me up onto his lap, as if I were a little child. I fell asleep there that evening, and hoped that I would never, ever wake up again.

CHAPTER FIFTEEN
Grandpa and me

I did get up the next day.

"What's the point of staying in bed?" I said to Grandpa, who heartily agreed.

"No, it's not worth staying in bed, lad."

But I wasn't happy, even if I might have looked like it after a couple of days. I went round trying to smile when someone was kind to me, because they all were, but inside I was just sad. Sometimes I stopped what I was doing and wondered how everything could change so quickly. Only a short time ago, Mathildewick Cove had been full of Auntie Granny's waffles and Lena's noise, and then suddenly almost everything I cared about had completely vanished. I had nobody to go to school with, nobody except Krølla to play with and nobody to sit at the ropeway window with. Instead I had a big, painful lump inside me, which would never disappear. I felt the lump was there mostly because Lena had left. That had changed everything. Trees weren't for climbing in any more, and my feet wouldn't run. She must have had something to do with food, too, because suddenly nothing tasted of anything. It made no difference if I ate bread with liver paste or ice cream. I almost wondered if I should stop eating. When I told Grandpa, he suggested that I should start eating boiled cabbage and cod liver oil.

"Seize the day, lad!"

Grandpa was now the best thing in my life.

He understood everything, without going on at me. Plus he was missing someone too. Everyone was sad. We missed Auntie Granny, and we missed Lena, and we missed Lena's mum. But it was Grandpa and me who were saddest. The whole day was full of sadness, from when we got up to when we went to bed.

When a whole week had passed and I'd experienced the first Friday without Lena, Grandpa and I were sitting at his small kitchen table, listening to the wind. I had been to school and walked there and back alone. When I came home, I was drenched with sleet and tears. Grandpa was the only one in, and he'd just made hot coffee. He gave me ten lumps of sugar and half a cup of coffee. There's no stopping Grandpa. Ten lumps of sugar!

I told him about my day. The boys in my class thought it was more boring at school now that Lena had left. The class had been quiet and strange, and not nearly as perfect as Kai-Tommy thought it would be without girls. I didn't say anything else for a while and picked at the sugar cubes. Thinking that Lena was never going to be in my class again was so sad that my stomach tied itself in knots.

"Grandpa, I miss her dreadfully," I said in the end, starting to cry again.

Grandpa looked at me seriously and said that missing people is the best sad feeling there is.

"You see, Trille lad, if you're sad because you miss someone, then that means you care about that person. And caring about someone is the best thing there is. We carry the people we miss inside us." He put his hand to his chest with a thump.

"Oh…" I said, pulling my sleeve across my eyes. "But, Grandpa, you can't play with people who are in there," I sighed, thumping my hand on my own chest.

Grandpa nodded heavily. He understood.

We didn't say any more, Grandpa and I. The wind whirled around the buildings, making enough noise. I didn't want to go out tobogganing by myself.

When I went back upstairs, Mum had made my favourite meal for dinner. It was the third time that week. Maybe I should've told her that I couldn't taste anything, but I decided not to. By the time I went to bed, it felt as if I had strained my smiling muscles. They were completely exhausted.

"Dear God, please give me back my sense of taste," I prayed.

The sad lump in my stomach meant that I couldn't sleep. I lay there listening to the horrible weather instead. Suddenly there was a bang on the windowpane.

"Help!" I mumbled, sitting up in bed, afraid.

There was another bang. I wished I still had Jesus above my bed! I was just about to run through to Mum and Dad's room when someone half-whispered and half-shouted:

"Come on, open the window, you dozy dormouse."

I sprang up and practically flew across to the window.

There was Lena, standing outside. In the middle of the night.

"Smoking haddocks! I thought I'd have to smash the window before you heard me," she said in irritation when I opened it.

I didn't say anything. Lena was standing outside my window with her rucksack on her back and her knitted hat on her head, and it felt like I hadn't seen her for a hundred years. She didn't say anything for a while either. She just looked at me in my pyjamas.

"It's cold," she said at last.

*   *   *

Shortly afterwards we were sitting in the kitchen drinking hot water. It was the quietest thing we could think of. Lena hadn't taken off her hat. She'd run away hours ago and was so cold that her teeth were chattering.

"I'll move into the hay barn," she said.

"Into the hay barn? Our hay barn?"

Lena nodded. And then a sob came out of her. I could see that she was struggling to look normal. For a long time she sat like that with a very strange look on her face, but eventually the tears came anyway. She was crying. Lena Lid, who never cries!

"Lena," I said, brushing the tears from her cheek. I didn't know what else I should do; she might strike out or something if I tried to hug her.

"Have you got a sleeping bag or haven't you?" she asked, a little severely.

"I have."

When I went back to bed, I was the only one
who knew that my best friend had moved back
to Mathildewick Cove. She was lying out in the
barn, wrapped up in a blanket, a sleeping bag and
the hay. And even if it was creepy to sleep in a
dark barn all alone, she probably slept like a log,
because the picture of Jesus was lying next to her
in the hay. I'd never been part of anything so secret
before. And I'd never been so happy.

CHAPTER SIXTEEN
The toboggan crash and a flying chicken

The next morning, I didn't remember immediately what had happened during the night. I just knew that I was happy. And when I did remember, I thought I must have dreamt it. I got up like a shot. The wind had stopped blowing and the fjord lay there light blue and smooth as a mirror. Everything was so bright with the snow, the sun and the sea; I'd never seen anything like it.

Mum was talking on the phone when I came downstairs. Nobody noticed me running outside. I bounded over to the hay barn. It was so cold that my footprints didn't show in the icy snow, and my heart was beating so lightly that I think I could have flown if I'd tried.

When there's such good weather outside, rays of sunlight come streaming into the hay barn, making it look like a church. I made my way to the far corner, furthest from the door, where Lena had been lying behind a stack of dry hay. The sleeping bag and the blanket were there. The picture of Jesus, too. But not Lena.

"Lena?" I whispered nervously.

What if I had dreamt it after all?

"Up here!" she said.

I looked up. Lena was sitting on the top beam, right under the roof. And then she jumped.

She fell and fell and landed next to me in the

hay without being hurt in the slightest. I smiled.
So did Lena.

"I've fallen off so many high places this year that it's become second nature. There's nothing I don't dare to do," she said proudly. "Oh, I'm so hungry!"

Walking back from the barn, I wished that I knew how to make scrambled eggs. That would be something very good to give to someone who had run away.

Grandpa was coming from the other barn and looked at me, surprised.

"You're a happy lad!"

"Well, you've got to try and smile when the weather's as good as this!" I said, clearing my throat.

Not even Grandpa could find out about this!

Mum had finished on the phone. She and Dad were sitting at the kitchen table. Steam was rising from their coffee, and the morning sun lit up the whole room.

"Trille, come and sit down," said Mum.

I didn't want to, but I did anyway. My parents looked at me seriously.

"I've just been speaking to Lena's mother. Lena wasn't in her bed this morning."

I turned the plate in front of me.

"Do you know where she is?" asked Dad.

"No," I said, starting to make some sandwiches.

They fell silent for a long moment.

"Trille," Mum said eventually, "Lena's mother is terribly worried. Everybody's looking for her. The police too. Do you know where she is?"

"No!" I shouted, slamming my hands on the table, because now I was so angry that I could have smashed up a house. Nobody was going to take Lena back to town! Even if all the police in the world came to Mathildewick Cove, Lena wasn't going to leave again. I stomped out of the kitchen in a fury. Grown-ups should never have been invented. Carrying on like this, taking children here and there when they didn't want to go!

I realized that everyone was going to start searching for Lena. Oh, why did everything have to be so difficult? Wasn't there a safe hide-out somewhere? I thought about everywhere in Mathildewick Cove, and I couldn't think of a single place.

"The cabin," I mumbled to myself in the end.

It would have to be the cabin.

When nobody was watching, I started putting together essentials in a plastic bag. Matches, a loaf of bread, butter, thick socks, rope, a shovel and the cabin keys. I moved quickly. Last of all, I took my toboggan out from its place under the steps and put everything I'd gathered on it, with a blanket on top. Now all I had to do was smuggle Lena out too!

"Where are you going, Trille?" Dad asked as I was putting on my snowsuit.

"I thought I'd go tobogganing and have some fun," I answered angrily.

And then I went down to the hay barn. I put the toboggan inside the door.

Lena had caught one of the hens.

"What are you going to do with her?" I asked, spotting that it was Number Seven.

Lena told me that she wasn't planning to starve – despite me bringing her so little food. At least hens lay the odd egg now and then. I shrugged and told her everything. Lena looked away for a moment.

"Yes," she said eventually. "I'll move into the cabin."

Her voice was strangely deep.

"But they'll see us when we go uphill, Trille," she said.

I nodded. There were just bare slopes all the way up to Hillside Jon's farm.

"You'll just have to pull us," said Lena with a smile, and, hey presto, she and Number Seven disappeared under the blanket on the toboggan, together with the bread and the butter and all the rest.

"And you mustn't make it look like it's heavy or they'll become suspicious!" she ordered.

Suspicious indeed! They had probably become suspicious a long while ago. At least, Grandpa had. He glanced out from below the balcony as I pulled the toboggan out of the barn. I gritted my teeth, wound the string one more time round my hand and set off.

Lena's not large, as I've said, but strangely it was still hard-going. I pulled and pulled so much I was sweating, while trying to make it look as if I were pulling the lightest toboggan in the world. But it was not the lightest toboggan in the world. It was one of the heaviest.

"Giddy up!" said Lena now and then, from under the blanket.

Thank goodness for the icy snow. I had never seen anything like it! There wasn't a trace of me or the toboggan.

We'd never taken the toboggan all the way up to Hillside Jon's place before. Not once. We would never have managed, at least not Lena. She only likes downhill slopes and thinks we should've built a toboggan lift in Mathildewick Cove long ago. Besides, it's already high enough for tobogganing long before you get to Hillside Jon's farmyard. If I hadn't been pulling my best friend, then I would never have made it. But Lena had come back. I couldn't stand the thought that she might disappear again.

Now and then I turned round to see if anyone was following us. Grandpa was next to the hay barn. He became smaller and smaller the further up we went. Eventually he was just a tiny dot. When I was finally able to lean against the wall up at Hillside, he was hardly even a dot any more.

"Lena, look at the view," I panted.

"I can see it," said Lena, sticking her head out from under the blanket. Number Seven clucked angrily from within.

Lena and I looked at our cove from above – at Mathildewick, our kingdom. The sun had disappeared behind the mountains, turning the whole sky beyond the fjord pink. There wasn't a ripple on the sea. Smoke rose from the chimney at our house. And even though it wasn't that late, the sky had teased out a star.

"What are you thinking about?" I asked, completely exhausted and absorbed by the view and big thoughts.

Lena rested her head on her hand.

"I'm thinking," she said in an hoarse voice, "I'm thinking that it's scandalous."

"Scandalous?"

"Scandalous, yep. Here we are, up at Hillside, higher than we've ever been before, with totally amazing ice on the snow. We've got a hen and a toboggan with us, but we can't go sledging!"

She shouted the last part.

I scratched my head.

"But, Lena, don't you want to go and stay in the cabin?"

My knees shook from exhaustion. Lena lay completely still. Winter made the whole world look calm.

"I want to stay in Mathildewick Cove!" said Lena with feeling. "And I want to go tobogganing," she added, getting up slowly and determinedly from under the blanket.

Before I could gather my thoughts, Lena had

turned the toboggan on its head, leaving the bread and butter in a heap on the snow. She sat well forward, so that there was space for me too. Lena and I hadn't been tobogganing together once this winter. We'd been too sad.

"Sit down then! You don't want to just stand there now you've pulled the toboggan all that way, do you? Besides, someone's got to hold the hen!"

Lena's eyes narrowed. I looked down the slope. The snow was sparkling. Who in their right mind would say no to a ride like this? I held tightly to Lena's waist with one hand, holding Number Seven closely with the other.

"Yee-ha!" we shouted in chorus.

"I suppose you've never been completely normal, you two," Magnus said a few days later, when Lena and I had recovered enough to sit at the kitchen table and eat with the others.

"It was about blooming time that Trille got concussion," Lena said sharply. As for her, she'd begun to get used to it, she claimed. I smiled. I felt happy all the way down to my little toes. Our concussion didn't matter.

"What was that toboggan ride like, anyway?" Minda asked with interest. I shrugged. Neither Lena nor I could remember anything.

But Grandpa remembered it. He'd been standing by the hay barn and had seen the whole thing.

"Well, let me tell you, Minda. They flew as fast as a speeding magpie. I've never seen anything like it in my whole life!"

Lena chewed thoughtfully.

"Smoking haddocks! Why can't I remember it?" she said angrily.

And then she got Grandpa to tell us – for what must have been the tenth time – how he had seen Lena and me and Number Seven set off from

Hillside Jon's farm. Suffering sticklebacks, he'd thought when he saw us picking up more and more speed on the hard snow. He'd heard the hen clucking and us shouting "yee-ha" until we got to about halfway. Then the hen fell silent, and Lena and I began to shout "whaah" instead. We had good reason to do so, because although we hadn't built any jumps, we'd been going at such a speed that we'd shot off the bank of snow with enough momentum to fly all the way over the main road.

"And then they sailed in a beautiful arc – the little lass head-first into Krølla's snowman, Trille with his face smack into the hedge, the hen skywards and the toboggan *bang* into the side of the house!" Grandpa concluded by clapping his hands together to show the sound it had actually made.

"And then Mum came," said Lena with a smile.

"Yes, then your mum came, little lass, and everything was sorted out."

The others kept on talking, but I went inside myself and was just happy. Lena wasn't my neighbour any more. She wasn't going to be my neighbour for a long time. She'd moved in with us instead! See what grown-ups can do when they set their minds to it.

After we'd recovered from the toboggan crash, I'd asked Mum if there was anything she could conjure up.

"Lena's mum and I have done some magic," Mum had answered. "We've cast a spell so that Lena will stay here with us until the summer, while her mum finishes her course."

"Abracadabra!" said Lena Lid, smiling.

CHAPTER SEVENTEEN
Hillside Jon and Hillside Molly

Having Lena at my house was even better than having her as a neighbour, although I wished she would give me back the picture of Jesus. It hung in her room, above the bed she'd been given.

"You'll get it back eventually, Trille," said Mum when I mentioned it to her. "Maybe Lena needs the picture at the moment."

"Yes, but now she's moved back to Mathildewick Cove, she's doing fine, isn't she?" I said.

Then Mum explained that, even if Lena didn't say anything, she must definitely be missing her mother. Especially when she went to bed in the evening.

"But she never says so," I argued.

"No, but does Lena usually say things like that?" asked Mum.

I thought for a bit, then shook my head. There are lots of things that Lena doesn't say.

"She's never told me that I'm her best friend," I said to Mum. "Do you think I am?"

Mum smiled. "Yes, I think so."

"But you can't be completely sure," I said.

No, you could never be completely sure if she didn't say so. Mum had to agree with that.

I didn't think Lena could be all that upset now, though.

"Isn't it great that I've moved in?" she kept on saying, grinning widely.

"Goodness gracious me, yes," Grandpa answered. "Trille and I thought it was pretty tame in Mathildewick Cove during that week when you weren't here."

In the afternoons, Lena and I had so much fun with Grandpa that we couldn't get back from school quickly enough. One day when we had come back and thrown our satchels under the balcony, Grandpa asked us if we wanted to go with him up to Hillside Jon's farm. The snow had disappeared, so we could cycle instead of tobogganing.

But cycling up to Hillside Jon's, while trying to keep up with Grandpa on his "super-duper-tuned" moped, was almost as tiring as pulling Lena all the way up there on the toboggan. Grandpa had the moped at full throttle and he laughed at us trailing behind. After that day, Lena and I gave Hillside Jon a new name: Hilltop Jon.

When Hilltop Jon was young, he was a sailor, and he lost one of his eyes in an accident. Since then, he's worn a black pirate's patch.

"I only see half of the world, and thank God for that," he tends to say.

Children are often scared of him because of the eye patch, but Lena and I both know that Hilltop Jon isn't dangerous. On the contrary, there are a lot of good things about him, and the best of all is Hillside Molly, his horse. In summer she grazes at the edge of the forest, and in winter she eats inside her stable.

"That mare is so intelligent that she can practically whinny hymn verses," Grandpa says.

When we finally got up there, Grandpa and Hilltop Jon sat on the steps drinking coffee, while Lena and I ran into the stable.

"She's quite an old horse," said Lena, tilting her head in the semi-darkness.

"She's intelligent," I said.

"How do you know that? Can you neigh?"

No, I couldn't. I just knew, but it was no good trying to explain that to Lena.

We stayed with Hillside Molly for a long while. We stroked her and talked to her, and Lena gave her a boiled sweet. I decided that she had to be the best horse in all the world.

"The horse ate a sweet," I told Grandpa when we got back to the moped.

"That was probably the last sweet she'll ever have," said Grandpa, tightening his helmet.

"What do you mean?" I asked in surprise, but by then Grandpa had started the engine and couldn't hear anything.

When we got home and he'd finally stopped the engine, I ran over and grabbed his hand.

"What do you mean, her 'last sweet'?"

Grandpa muttered a little, but then he said that Hilltop Jon was so old that he was going to a retirement home, and Molly was so old that nobody wanted her. "Getting old is rubbish," Grandpa mumbled angrily, shutting the door in my face.

"What are they going to do with Molly, then?" I shouted through the closed door.

Grandpa didn't answer. He sat indoors being angry because people and horses and grandpas get old. But Lena answered, loud and clear:

"There are no retirement homes for horses. Don't you get it? She's going to be put down."

I stared at Lena for a long moment. Then I yelled, as loudly as she normally does:

"THEY CAN'T!"

"Can't," repeated Krølla seriously.

I told Mum and Dad too. I cried and said that they couldn't put down horses that were as intelligent as Molly.

"But, Trille dear, we send sheep to be slaughtered every single year, and you never make such a fuss about that!" said Mum, trying to dry my tears.

"Molly's no sheep!"

They didn't understand a thing!

The next day, Molly was all I could think about. That good-natured horse who had never done anything wrong to anyone but who was going to die. During our Maths lesson I almost started crying. That would have been pretty embarrassing! I glanced across at Lena. She was sitting, looking out of the window. There are no retirement homes for horses, she'd said.

Suddenly I stood up, tipping over my chair.

"Ellisiv, Lena and I have got to have the rest of the day off," I said, distressed.

Lena had no idea what I was talking about. Still, she stuffed her Maths book into her bag determinedly, put on a serious face and said:

"It's a matter of life and death!"

And while Ellisiv and the others watched in astonishment, Lena and I stormed out of the classroom with our satchels half-open.

"Have you got ants in your pants?" Lena puffed as we ran through the woods on our way home.

"We're going to start a retirement home for horses!" I shouted enthusiastically.

Lena stopped dead in her tracks. Apart from some birds singing and us puffing after all that running, it was completely quiet. I looked at her anxiously. What if she didn't like the idea? But then came the beaming response:

"What an incredibly brilliant idea to come up with something like that right in the middle of Maths, Trille!"

Grandpa was the only one who was home. That was good. He was the only one who would be any help. I sat down next to him beneath the balcony.

"We can keep Molly in the old stables, Grandpa. She can live there. Imagine how happy Hilltop Jon will be if he doesn't have to send her to the abattoir! I'll cut the grass and rake it up and dry it and look after her and feed her, and Lena can help. Right, Lena?"

Lena nodded. Well, she might as well help a bit with that old horse, she said. I could see that she was happy because of missing Maths.

"And maybe you could help too, Grandpa?" I asked weakly, hardly daring to look at him. Grandpa rubbed his tanned, wrinkled hands on his knees and looked thoughtfully out to sea.

"For example, maybe you could be the grown-up who gives us permission," I said, even more weakly.

It was difficult to ask for something like this. I could feel that the tears were on their way again, and I fought to hold them back. Grandpa fixed his gaze on me.

"Oh, suffering sticklebacks, all right! There's no reason young Trille and the little lass from next door couldn't cope with looking after a horse," he said eventually.

There were two good reasons for riding in the moped box this time, Grandpa said. Firstly, we had to make it up to Hilltop Jon before he sent Molly away on the slaughter lorry. Secondly, we had to make it up to Hilltop Jon before Grandpa had time to think again.

"Because right now I must be off my head!" he said.

We braked suddenly in the farmyard up at Hillside. There was a car there. It was Vera Johansen's. Hilltop Jon is her uncle. She was helping him with the packing and the cleaning before he went to the retirement home. As for Hilltop Jon himself, he was sitting on a chair, looking helpless. Grandpa stuck his hands into his boiler-suit pockets and nodded silently to his best friend.

"The young lad's got something he wants to ask you," he said, clearing his throat and pushing me across the floor.

"I…" I whispered. "I was just wondering whether I could take on Hillside Molly. We're going to start a retirement home for horses. Lena, Grandpa and me…"

It turned so quiet that you could have heard a pin drop, and I barely dared to look at Hilltop Jon. He brushed his hand quickly over his good eye.

"Bless you, boy," he said. "But Molly left on the ferry twenty minutes ago."

As I stood in front of Hilltop Jon, looking into his sad eye, I thought I'd never be happy ever again, just like the day when Lena left. But then Lena herself piped up.

"Hello? Are we going to start a retirement home or aren't we?" she said indignantly, pulling me by the jacket. "Surely a horse can't be finished off that quickly!"

And she ran outside. All Grandpa and I could do was follow her. As we were starting the moped, Hilltop Jon came tottering out onto the step. He waved at us, with many different emotions showing on his face.

"Drive, Grandpa! Drive like a madman!" I shouted.

And Grandpa drove. I understood for the first time why Mum didn't want us to sit in that box. Even Lena looked a little scared as we went down the hill. We were going so fast and bumping around so terribly that I bit my tongue three times. But still we weren't going fast enough.

"Keep going! The ferry's put down the barrier!" I shouted.

"Come back, you stupid ferry!" shouted Lena.

We jumped out of the box and waved our arms.

The captain spotted us, and maybe he saw that Grandpa was waving too, because he came back. The ferry docked with a bang, and Able Seaman Birger let us aboard. Dad was on his lunch break and was nowhere to be seen.

"Maybe it's best if you don't tell Dad that we're here right now," I said to Able Seaman Birger.

"Why not?" he asked.

"It's a surprise," said Lena. "It's his birthday," she added.

Able Seaman Birger looked at Grandpa, and Grandpa nodded sincerely.

"Yes, you look after that young lad, he's forty-four today," he said, giving Birger such a slap on the back that it made his ticket bag jangle. I looked at Grandpa and Lena in shock. What were they talking about?

"Sometimes it's all right to tell white lies, Trille, my boy," said Grandpa. "And this will be just great for your father. Maybe Able Seaman Birger will cobble together some cake and a present!"

I don't think it had ever taken the ferry so long to get to town. I stood peering over the ferry door the whole way, and it felt like we were never getting any closer. But with every second that passed, Hillside Molly was getting closer to the abattoir.

"We're never going to make it in time," I said. "I just want to jump overboard and swim!"

"If you're going to splash about in the middle of the fjord without a lifejacket, then you'll definitely never make it in time!" Lena helpfully informed me.

Grandpa looked at his watch.

When we finally reached the town, Grandpa drove even faster, but he threw the woollen blanket over Lena and me so that nobody would see us. Especially not the police. I lay there thinking about all the forbidden things we'd done that day: skiving our Maths lesson, lying to Able Seaman Birger, starting a retirement home without permission and riding in the moped box down the hill and through town. I felt really bad about it. But then I pictured Hillside Molly.

"Dear God, please let us make it!"

"Wait here," Grandpa said strictly when we got to the abattoir.

And then he tramped inside in his boiler suit and wooden shoes. Lena and I stood waiting in the middle of a large car park. So this was where we sent sheep every autumn, I thought, and my stomach began to hurt a little. We couldn't hear a sound from inside.

"Maybe she's already been turned into sausages," Lena said after a while. "Just waiting for the mayonnaise."

"Stop it," I mumbled angrily.

But Hillside Molly had got there almost an hour before us. She was most likely no longer alive. Why wasn't Grandpa coming out? Maybe he couldn't bear to tell me? I tried not to cry, but I had tears in my eyes. Lena kicked her shoe on the asphalt and pretended that she didn't see.

Then the door finally opened, and out came Grandpa – without Molly.

"Oh no!" I shouted.

"Now, now, Trille. I couldn't exactly lead her through their offices, could I? We've got to go round to the other side to collect her."

We had made it after all! But as Grandpa said, it was a close shave. Suddenly there I was with my own horse in an enormous car park. I couldn't believe that anyone could be so happy!

We made quite a funny procession as we strolled back through town. Grandpa went first on his moped. I followed, leading Molly, and finally along came Lena, who kept announcing that it looked like Molly was about to poo.

Molly didn't poo until we got to the ferry queue. We took our places behind a black Mercedes – Grandpa on his moped, then me with the horse and finally Lena.

"Now she's pooing like there's no tomorrow!" Lena shouted joyfully.

People looked at us strangely, and I was glad I had found myself such a wise and gentle horse who stood there so calmly, otherwise it would probably have been mayhem.

Actually, fairly soon it was mayhem, because Dad had finished his break. He was standing on the bow as the ferry moored. When he spotted us, he gaped so widely that I could see his wisdom teeth all the way from the shore. In his astonishment he forgot to wave the Mercedes and the other cars aboard. They started up anyway, and we followed them towards Dad, who was standing in the middle of the deck with a birthday party crown sticking out of his pocket. The Mercedes rumbled by first, then Grandpa chugged by, then Hillside Molly and I walked on board, with me not daring to look at Dad, and afterwards came Lena, smiling broadly. She likes a commotion.

Dad sold the Mercedes a ticket first, so he could collect his thoughts. Then he came to Grandpa on his moped. Dad was red in the face and had probably planned an entire speech. But Grandpa clambered off his moped, drew out his wallet and said:

"One pensioner, two children and a horse, please."

"And many happy returns of the day!" added Lena.

*   *   *

That day, Dad said he was going to be a pensioner long ahead of his time because of us, but Lena said it didn't matter: he could get a place at our retirement home too. Even though it was mainly for horses.

CHAPTER EIGHTEEN
Lena and I play World War II

"You can't just get yourself a horse," said
Mum, even though that was exactly what I'd
done. She and Dad were pretty angry. If it hadn't
been for Grandpa, I think we would have had to
take Molly back, but Grandpa sorted it out. And
even if they pretended otherwise, I noticed that
my parents gradually came to think it was a very
good and well-behaved horse we had down in the
old stables.

Life returned to its usual course again. March was approaching, and I had become used to having both the horse and Lena around. At the weekends, Lena went to town to her mum's, and often, in the afternoons, her mum came to visit Mathildewick Cove. I thought about it every day, about how happy I was that Lena hadn't moved away. It was so good not being lonely and sad! For a long time nothing went out of control either. We behaved like a couple of angels for several weeks, Lena and I, after that business with Hillside Molly.

"It's enough to make me nervous," Dad said one day at the dinner table. "It's not normal for it to be so peaceful in Mathildewick Cove."

I'm not certain, but I think it was probably that comment which gave Lena such a brilliant idea when we were clearing the table afterwards. She suddenly stopped and stood there looking at our radio.

"Let's bury it, Trille."

"Bury the radio?"

"Yes, like Auntie Granny told us," said Lena. "We'll bury it and pretend that it's the War."

It was good to do something that Auntie Granny had told us about. She would probably like it, from where she was sitting up in heaven. Still, it was so forbidden that my whole body quivered.

But Lena said that we should do it. Then we'd really understand what war was like, and it had to be a good idea to learn about that.

So all the other people in Mathildewick Cove became German soldiers, even though they didn't know it. Lena and I were the only Norwegians, and we tiptoed around like two spies from the Resistance.

"They'll send us to a camp if they catch us," said Lena.

We dug a hole next to the chicken run. It was hard work, but it was big and deep when we'd finished. So big and deep that we decided to gather together all the radios in Mathildewick Cove.

People have a lot more radios these days than they had when Auntie Granny was young. There was the radio in the bathroom, the stereo system in the living room, Magnus's portable radio, Minda's CD player with radio tuner and Grandpa's big old radio.

"Wow," I said several times when we realized how many there were.

"Yes, it's quite a lot, but it's pointless to have dug such a big hole if we're not going to fill it right up," Lena decided.

We must be pretty good at this war business, Lena and I, because we got hold of all the radios without being spotted. It was a huge collection. We even managed to haul the big stereo system over to the hole without anyone noticing.

"Shall we bury them now?" said Lena as we dropped Magnus's portable radio onto the top of the pile.

"Won't they be ruined?" I asked.

Lena thought that radios must be fairly tough if they'd done this during the War, when everything was so terrible. We put a bin bag on top and some soil above that. And then off we ran to spy on the German soldiers.

First we sat behind the kitchen door, watching Mum search high and low for her radio. Then we peeked down at Grandpa, who was standing in the middle of the room, scratching his head.

"Is something up, Grandpa?" I asked innocently.

"I've gone senile, Trille lad. I remember so clearly that I had a radio here this morning, but now it's vanished. And who could've moved that rickety old contraption if I didn't do it myself?"

Lena vanished like a fly. When I found her

again, she was lying behind the barn, rolling around with laughter.

But soon the German soldiers began conferring. Mum spoke with Grandpa, and Grandpa spoke with Minda, and Minda spoke with Magnus, and Magnus spoke with Dad. They all ended up in our kitchen, talking about the missing radios. Lena and I sat on the attic stairs, listening.

"Do you think they're going to suspect us?" Lena whispered.

"Yes, actually," I mumbled.

We decided to escape. The Norwegians did that during the war; they went to Sweden and became refugees. We would have to be quick, because now the soldiers had begun looking for us.

"There should be a bounty on your head, Trille!" I heard Magnus shouting somewhere, not terribly far away.

"We can take Hillside Molly!" I whispered.

How Lena and I managed to get into the old stables and up onto the horse without anyone noticing is a miracle.

"We're clearly experts at escaping," said Lena as we sat up on the horse, riding bareback. I clutched onto Molly's mane. Lena clutched onto me, saying "Giddy up".

We took the shortcut we'd taken on the moped when the Balthazar Gang were after us. We weren't going fast, even with Lena endlessly saying "Giddy up". Hillside Molly is no racehorse, to put it kindly. She's a hillside mare.

"Smoking haddocks, what a rubbish horse," Lena moaned, annoyed. "We've got to take cover somewhere!"

"We're going to see Hilltop Jon," I said. "It's not far, and then we can see how he's getting on!"

The retirement home was completely quiet when we got there. Lena looked at the big building. She thought it was the spitting image of Sweden. She'd been to Sweden once, when she was two.

"Shall we tie up Molly here?" she said, pointing at a sign.

Usually when Lena and I visit the retirement home, we come with our class for a performance or something. It was different being just the two of us, without our recorders. But we found the lounge where Hilltop Jon was sitting, looking out of the window with his one eye. I think he was missing Hillside.

"Ahem," Lena said loudly.

Hilltop Jon was pleasantly surprised to see us. I explained as best as I could about the radios and the Germans and everything, and he understood. But there were several other people in the lounge, and some of them understood a little *too* well. For example, one old woman called Anna, who thought the War was still on, and that the German soldiers really were after Lena and me.

Before we knew it, Lena and I found ourselves huddled between skirts and blouses in Anna's wardrobe. She put a chair in front of it and sat guarding us.

"No soldier alive can get past me!" shouted Anna.

Neither could Lena and I. I was beginning to feel a little sceptical about the whole war thing, but Lena chuckled away happily in the darkness.

After a while, Anna suddenly shouted, "There's nobody in the wardrobe!" I pressed my whole body against the door so a small gap opened up. I peeped out. Dad, Grandpa, Minda and Magnus had come in. Then Hilltop Jon forced his way past them and took a banana from the bedside table, pretending that it was a pistol. It was such a strange sight that both Lena and I started laughing. Everyone laughed, actually, except Anna. She didn't think it was funny in the slightest and defended us as well as she could. It was only when Dad went out into the lounge and sat down at the piano and Grandpa asked her to join him in a waltz that she forgot what she was doing and let Lena and me out of the cupboard.

"How did you find us?" I asked.

"You know, it's funny, but when you see a horse standing outside a retirement home, you feel that you're getting warm!" Dad said angrily from the piano stool.

"It's not easy to park that animal," Lena answered gruffly.

Hilltop Jon's eye opened wide. "Have you brought Hillside Molly, dear children?"

I don't think I've ever seen an old man so happy.

We stayed a good while at the retirement home that evening. And when we left, I promised to come with Molly and visit often. But first Mum gave Lena and me our punishment. For three whole afternoons we had to pick up stones in the field where this year's cabbages were going to be planted.

CHAPTER NINETEEN
The fire

Green shoots were appearing and spring was getting closer. I could feel it throughout my body. Every morning I stood at my window looking out, and felt that it was almost spring now. One afternoon, Lena and I took Krølla with us to show her.

First we went down to the barn.

"Soon lambs will be coming out of the ewes' bums," Lena explained, while I stroked my favourite ewe on the head. She was as fat as a beach ball. Krølla grinned and gave her some hay.

"And then the grass outside will become green, and we can let the lambs out into the fields. Do you remember last year, Krølla?"

"Yep," said Krølla, but I think she was lying.

Afterwards we went into the garden, and stood underneath the pear tree. No snowdrops had come out there yet, but I pointed and explained where they were going to pop up.

"They might come in the next week or so," I said, and Krølla promised to check.

Lena and I explained everything about spring to Krølla. It's good being a big brother.

"And then it'll be the Midsummer festival again," I said. "And we'll light a big bonfire down on the shore."

"Then Grandpa will spray the muck!" Krølla laughed.

She remembered that.

"But who's going to be the Midsummer bride and groom?" I said, mostly to myself, feeling a twinge inside me.

Auntie Granny was no longer here.

"Not the two of us, anyway," Lena blurted out.

Grandpa was sitting under the balcony with his fishing nets. Krølla told him that we were looking at the spring.

"Yes, spring's certainly on its way, but it's going to be rough weather this evening, I tell you," said Grandpa, scrunching up his eyes a little as he looked out across the fjord. It was very dark on the other side. It was so strange to be standing in the sun and the good weather in Mathildewick Cove, watching it rain elsewhere!

As a matter of fact, it wasn't long before it was tipping down in our cove too. We hurried inside and did indoor things for the rest of the day. When we went to bed, the thunder and lightning had started. I lay there for a long time listening to the thunderclaps. Deep inside I wished I could sneak into Lena's room and take down the picture of Jesus. I thought about how *she* didn't have to be afraid, while I was here feeling scared, when it was actually *my* picture. In the end the thunder was so loud that I couldn't stay in bed any more. I got up to go to Mum and Dad's room, just to ask if such loud crashes were normal.

Lena was standing in the corridor.

"Are you frightened?" she asked quickly when I came out of my room.

I shrugged. "Are you?"

Lena shook her head. And then I began to feel angry. She had my picture of Jesus, and besides, I was sure that she was fibbing.

"You are! What else would you be standing here in the corridor for?" I asked.

Lena crossed her arms in front of her chest, making a noise. "I'm going outside."

"Outside?"

"Outside. Yes. I'm going to sleep on the balcony, so I can hear those thunder-farts properly!"

A tingle started inside me, but before my knees had time to start shaking, I said:

"So am I!"

I was so frightened! Even though you couldn't see it on Lena's face, I'm sure that she was frightened too. She had to be. The thunder was so loud that the balcony shook. We were soaking wet in a few minutes, even sitting under the roof inside our sleeping bags. Now and then, forks of lightning zigzagged across the sky, lighting up everything as if it were the middle of the day. It rained and poured and thundered and boomed so much that it was really terrifying. I'd never experienced such powerful thunder. Every clap was stronger than the one before. I ended up putting my hands over my ears and closing my eyes. Lena sat next to me like a ship's figurehead, her mouth forming a straight line. And suddenly I realized that she was probably missing her mother. I let my hands drop. Poor Lena! I was just about to say something when a bolt of lightning and a clap of thunder came almost together. The light and the noise were so strong that Lena and I squeezed ourselves together and buried our faces in our sleeping bags.

"We're crazy!" I shouted. "We've got to go indoors, Lena!"

Lena didn't answer. She was on her feet already.

"Trille, the old stables are on fire!"

I shook off my sleeping bag and pulled myself up. Fire!

"Molly!" I shouted and began to run.

Behind me, I heard Lena yelling into the house as only she can yell. And then she screamed at me:

"Trille, don't go in there!"

But I didn't listen. In the middle of the lightning and rain and fire, Molly was in the stables. I had to get her out. At the moment the flames were just under the roof. I tore open the door. There was smoke everywhere, but I knew exactly where she was standing.

"There, there," I said, grabbing hold of her mane. "Come along, girl."

She just stood there. Totally frozen to the spot. I stroked her and spoke to her and pulled, but Molly stood stock-still. She wouldn't move. It was as if she wanted to be burnt in there. Didn't she realize that she had to get out?

I started to cry.

"Come on!" I shouted, tugging her mane as hard as I could. The horse kicked her hooves, but stayed where she was. It was becoming difficult to breathe, and I could feel I was about to panic.

Then Lena came. Through the smoke. She gripped me by my arm so hard that it hurt, and tried to pull me out like I was pulling Molly.

"The horse!" I wailed, no longer able to see anything.

"Get out, Trille! The roof's collapsing!" Lena's voice was angry.

"The horse. She won't budge," I cried, standing just as still as Molly.

Then Lena let go of my hand.

"That horse is as stupid as a cow!" she shouted, and then very quietly she moved right next to Molly's ear. There was the sound of cracking and creaking.

"BOO!" Lena yelled suddenly.

Molly galloped out at top speed, making me lose my balance and fall backwards. Lena was almost out of the stable when she spotted me.

"Trille!" she shouted fearfully, turning round as quick as a flash. Suddenly a burning beam came falling down from the ceiling.

"Trille!" Lena shouted again.

I couldn't answer. I felt just like Molly – scared stiff. The burning beam lay between me and the door.

Then there she was. Lena jumped over the beam like a little kangaroo. Her thin fingers dug into my arm again. She gave an enormous pull and practically threw me towards the exit. In fact, I think she really did throw me. I dragged myself forward for the last stretch towards the open stable door. The next thing I remember is my cheek lying in wet grass, and strong hands pulling me all the way out of the stables.

My whole family was out in the rain, and there was shouting and yelling everywhere.

"Lena," I whispered. I couldn't see her anywhere. It was Mum who was holding me.

"Lena's in the stables!" I shouted, trying to get free. But Mum kept holding me. I kicked and shouted and cried, but I couldn't get free. I looked at the open door helplessly. Lena was inside! Lena was inside the fire…

Then Grandpa came staggering out of the flames with a big bundle in his hands. He sank down on his knees in exhaustion and laid Lena on the grass.

Hospitals. I don't like them. But they make people better. Here I was, all alone in front of a white door, on a hospital visit. I knocked. Under my arm I was carrying a box of chocolates. I'd swapped the ones that came in the box for pieces of milk chocolate.

"Come in!" came the shout from inside, as loud as a mixed choir.

Lena was sitting in bed reading an old Donald

Duck comic. She had a white bandage on her head, and her hair had been shaved off. Some of it had burnt off in the fire, and she had inhaled a lot of smoke, too. Otherwise Lena was OK. Everything had been all right in the end, but still it was strange to see her like this.

"Hi," I said, giving her the box of chocolates.

Lena wrinkled her nose. I quickly told her that there was milk chocolate inside.

"Do you want some strawberry jam?" she asked.

I certainly did. In her bedside drawer Lena had a whole stock of strawberry jam in small jars. She could get as many as she wanted, she explained. We ate strawberry jam and chocolate for a bit, while I asked Lena if her head hurt, and other things that you ask sick people about. Lena wasn't really hurting. Most of all she wanted to go home. But the doctor said she had to stay there for another day or two so they could keep an eye on her.

"Yes, that's probably a good idea," I said, understanding what they meant.

Above her bed hung my picture of Jesus.

"Lena," I mumbled after a while.

"Mm-hmm?"

"Thank you for saving me."

She didn't answer.

"It was brave."

"Pff," said Lena, looking to the side. "I did what I had to."

I thought about that. What she had to? But before I could think any more, Lena added:

"I didn't want my best friend to go up in smoke, did I?"

I was speechless for a long while.

"Am I your best friend?" I said eventually.

Lena gave me a strange look.

"Of course you are! Who else would it be? Kai-Tommy?"

A big stone melted somewhere inside my stomach. I had a best friend! Lena was sitting there with her head shaved and bandaged, licking the strawberry jam out of yet another jar. She had no idea how happy I was!

"I think my knees are going to shake a lot less from now on," I smiled.

Lena didn't think so.

"But it was brave of you to go in after that stupid horse," she admitted. "Oh, by the way, Trille, I've proposed," she added.

"Proposed? To who?"

And then Lena told me how, earlier that day, she'd been lying in her hospital bed, looking as if she were sleeping, while her mother and Isak sat on each side, watching over her. They were talking about love and about Lena and about Mathildewick Cove. Lena realized that Isak didn't really have anything against living in Mathildewick Cove,

if need be. He'd heard that it might be possible
to tidy up the cellar, he said.

"But they weren't getting to the point, Trille!"
said Lena. "So eventually I opened my eyes like
a flash of lightning."

"And then what?" I asked excitedly.

"And then I said, 'Isak, will you marry us?'"

"You did? What did he say?"

Lena gave me another strange look.

"He said yes, of course!"

She put a piece of chocolate in her mouth and
chuckled with satisfaction.

"You're going to have a dad, Lena!" I shouted
happily.

CHAPTER TWENTY

The Midsummer bride and groom

Everything was ready when Midsummer came round again. I stood at the wide-open window in my room, looking out across our kingdom. It was hard to believe that days like this existed, with the sun and the sea and the newly cut fields.

"Lena! We've got to go out!"

And even though it was the wedding day, with all the wedding fuss, we just slipped out into the summer, Lena and I. We were only causing havoc and getting in the way, anyway. It was better to be running races across the fields.

"Trille, you slowcoach," Lena huffed when we got down to the shore at exactly the same time.

I thought I was hardly a slowcoach, but I didn't say so. And then we went paddling and threw seaweed against the boathouse wall with a smack, because nothing makes as good a smacking noise as seaweed. Afterwards we hopped all the way across the rocks to Uncle Tor's, where Lena snuck on board the shark boat and stuck a dandelion into the cabin keyhole. The heifers were out grazing.

"Do you think it's possible to ride cattle?" Lena asked.

It is possible, we found out. Lena thought we could take bigger risks now that we had a doctor in the cove. And even though we'd promised

Uncle Tor never to borrow his heifers again without asking, we did. And everything went the same way it usually does. Very wrong.

But by the evening, Lena had been patched up and had cleaned off all the cow muck. She was even wearing a dress. It was the Midsummer festival *and* the wedding, so there was no limit to what she'd agree to.

"I do," said Isak when the church minister asked if he took Lena's mum to be his lawful wedded wife.

"I do," said Lena's mum when the minister asked her.

As for Lena, she said a massive, loud and booming "I DO", even though nobody asked her, because this wedding would never have taken place if it hadn't been for all her concussions.

* * *

The bonfire burnt serenely, the summer evening was mild and warm, and there were more people and music down on our shoreline than there had ever been before.

"Do you think the bride is prettier this year than last?" Grandpa asked me later that evening.

He was sitting on a rock with a cup of coffee, all dressed up smart, a short distance away from the others.

"Maybe a little," I confessed, because Lena's mum was the prettiest bride I'd ever seen.

"Hm," said Grandpa, pretending to be offended.

"Are you missing Auntie Granny today?" I asked.

"Maybe a little," Grandpa answered, turning his coffee cup around in his fingers.

I stood there looking at him for a while, feeling as if my heart were growing inside my chest so that there wasn't any more space. I wanted to give Grandpa all the good things in the whole world.

And all at once I knew what to do. Quietly, I crept away from the shore and up to the farm.

Grandpa's flat was half dark and peaceful. I clambered up onto the kitchen counter and stretched as high as I could. There it was, right up on top of the kitchen cupboard: Auntie Granny's waffle iron. I lifted it down and held it in my hands for a while. Then I went into Grandpa's bedroom. Inside his prayer book was a crumpled, faded piece of paper. *Waffle Hearts*, it read at the top, in old lady handwriting. That was what Auntie Granny's waffles were called.

I'm not very good at baking, but I followed the recipe exactly, and soon I had a large bowl of waffle batter. Just when I was about to start cooking, the door flew wide open like a thunderclap.

"What on earth are you doing here?" said Lena, looking at me suspiciously.

Then she caught sight of the waffle iron.

"Ohh…"

"Maybe you should go back down," I suggested, even though really I wanted Lena to stay. "Your mum's getting married and everything."

Lena stared at the waffle iron.

"Mum will be fine by herself," she decided, leaning against the door so that it slammed shut.

I'll never forget the night that Lena and I made waffle hearts for Grandpa while a real Midsummer bride and groom were celebrating their wedding on the shore. We sat on the kitchen counter, on each side of the waffle iron, saying almost nothing. The music and the happy voices buzzed in the background, making enough noise as it was. I poured the mixture, and Lena took out the waffle hearts.

"You can have your picture back now," Lena said suddenly. I spilled some mixture outside the waffle iron out of pure astonishment.

"Thank you," I said happily.

* * *

When we'd cooked almost all the mixture, Grandpa
came in. He was completely flabbergasted to see us
there. And even more flabbergasted when he saw
what we were doing.

"Surprise!" Lena shouted, so loudly that the
wallpaper almost came off the walls.

And then Grandpa, Lena and I ate waffle hearts
for the first time since Auntie Granny had died. I'm
sure that she was smiling down on us from heaven.
Grandpa smiled too.

"Trille lad and the little lass from next door,"
he said softly a couple of times, shaking his head
affectionately.

After seven rounds of waffles, Grandpa fell
asleep in his chair. He doesn't usually stay up so
late. Lena and I laid a blanket over him and crept
out. We climbed up into the cedar tree. On the
shore, the wedding party was still going on.

We could just glimpse the people down there in the light summer night.

"Now you've got a dad too, Lena," I said.

"Smoking haddocks, so I have!" She smiled cheerfully, scoffing down the last waffle heart.

And I've got a best friend, I thought happily.

Maria Parr is an outstanding Norwegian children's author. Her debut novel, *Vaffelhjarte (Waffle Hearts)*, has been translated into twenty-five different languages, and won France's Prix Sorcières in 2010, the Dutch Zilveren Griffel in 2008, and was shortlisted for Norway's prestigious Brage Prize. It has also been made into a popular children's television series in Norway. Her second novel, *Tonje Glimmerdal*, won the Brage Prize and the Norwegian Critics' Prize in 2009. Maria has a Master's degree in Nordic Languages and Literature and lives in Norway with her family.

Guy Puzey grew up in the Highlands of Scotland, just a short swim away from Norway. He began translating Norwegian literature in 2006, having studied the language at the University of Edinburgh. He completed his doctorate in 2011 and now works at the University as a course organizer and researcher, and has taught a number of courses, including Scandinavian linguistic history, children's literature and literary translation.

SHORTLISTED FOR THE MARSH AWARD
FOR CHILDREN'S LITERATURE IN TRANSLATION